Tessa's weary mind echoed Dominic's name....

Dear heaven, something strange and sensual had happened when she and Dominic looked into each other's eyes. She could still feel the heat that had thrummed through her body.

Dominic's dark, compelling eyes had held her immobile. She'd been so incredibly aware of him as a man, and she'd experienced a near-painful acknowledgement of her own femininity. Even her skin had tingled.

It had been unsettling, to say the least. She'd vowed years before to never again fall prey to a man's charm or masculine magnetism. She'd always been in control of her feelings, her emotions, her life.

Until now.

Until Dominic Bonelli.

"Oh, Tessa..." she said, shaking her head. Her slumbering womanliness was being awakened by the last man on earth she'd wish to have anything to do with.

Well, she was putting her femininity back to sleep. Somehow.

Dear Reader,

Special Edition's lineup for the month of July is sure to set off some fireworks in your heart! Romance always seems that much more wonderful and exciting in the hot days of summer, and our six books for July are sure to prove that! We begin with bestselling author Gina Ferris Wilkins and *A Match for Celia.* July's THAT SPECIAL WOMAN! goes looking for summertime romance and gets more than she bargained for in book two of Gina's series, THE FAMILY WAY.

Continuing the new trilogy MAN, WOMAN AND CHILD this month is Robin Elliott's *Mother at Heart.* Raising her sister's son as her own had been a joy for this single mother, but her little family seems threatened when the boy's real father surfaces... until she finds herself undeniably drawn to the man. Be sure to look for the third book in the series next month, *Nobody's Child,* by Pat Warren.

Father in Training by Susan Mallery brings you another irresistible hunk who can only be one of those HOMETOWN HEARTBREAKERS. Also continuing in July is Victoria Pade's A RANCHING FAMILY series. Meet Jackson Heller, of the ranching Heller clan, in *Cowboy's Kiss.* A man who's lost his memory needs tenderness and love to find his way in Kate Freiman's *Here To Stay.* And rounding out the month is a sexy and lighthearted story by Jane Gentry. In *No Kids or Dogs Allowed,* falling in love is easy for a single mom and divorced dad—until they find out their feuding daughters may just put a snag in their upcoming wedding plans!

A whole summer of love and romance has just begun from **Special Edition!** I hope you enjoy each and every story to come!

Sincerely,

Tara Gavin
Senior Editor

Please address questions and book requests to:
Silhouette Reader Service
U.S.: 3010 Walden Ave., P.O. Box 1325, Buffalo, NY 14269
Canadian: P.O. Box 609, Fort Erie, Ont. L2A 5X3

ROBIN ELLIOTT

MOTHER AT HEART

SPECIAL EDITION®

Published by Silhouette Books
America's Publisher of Contemporary Romance

For my mother, Olive Elliott,
for all and everything....
Thanks, Mom.

 SILHOUETTE BOOKS

ISBN 0-373-09968-1

MOTHER AT HEART

Copyright © 1995 by Joan Elliott Pickart

Printed in U.S.A.

ROBIN ELLIOTT

lives in a small, charming town in the high pine country of Arizona. She enjoys watching football, attending craft shows on the town square and gardening. Robin has published over sixty novels and also writes under her own name, Joan Elliott Pickart.

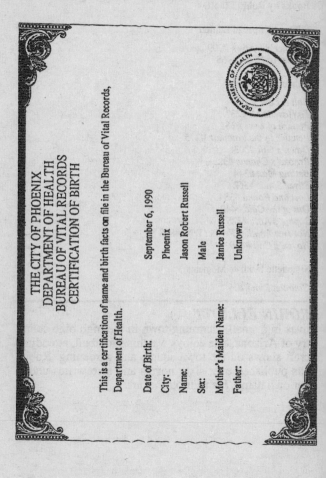

THE CITY OF PHOENIX
DEPARTMENT OF HEALTH
BUREAU OF VITAL RECORDS
CERTIFICATION OF BIRTH

This is a certification of name and birth facts on file in the Bureau of Vital Records, Department of Health.

Date of Birth: September 6, 1990

City: Phoenix

Name: Jason Robert Russell

Sex: Male

Mother's Maiden Name: Janice Russell

Father: Unknown

Prologue

Abby Thatcher laid her head on her folded arms and tried not to cry. Winthrop had hated tears, though God knew he'd handled enough weeping women during the forty years he'd practiced law in this small office in downtown Phoenix.

Exhaustion, combined with sorrow, had her feeling numb. But the numbness didn't make the ache in her heart go away. She raised her head and, taking a deep breath, straightened her thin shoulders and patted her salt-and-pepper hair. Indulging her grief wouldn't get the work done, and now, on top of everything else, she had to deal with the ineptitude of the temporary help she'd just dismissed. In two days, the silly woman hadn't been able to follow the simplest directions.

It had been only three days since Winthrop's funeral, but with all Abby had had to cope with since his fatal heart attack last week, it seemed more like three years.

She opened a file on her always-organized desk, wishing instead she could give way to her grief for the man she had loved for over four decades, the man who'd seen her only as his dedicated, organized and ever-so dependable secretary. There had never been any hope for her. Winthrop Ames, Esq., had been married to the law.

Her last official duty would be to close his office. Before she could, she had to make arrangements for his pending cases and dispose of a lifetime's accumulation of files, since he had no partners.

The half-dozen cartons along the oak-paneled wall of the small library would be picked up this afternoon by a messenger from the law firm one of Winthrop's clients had asked to assume his case. Yesterday, she'd directed the temp to mail several real estate files. Abby was still waiting to hear from other people she'd spoken with regarding their cases, and had letters to write to Winthrop's remaining clients.

But before another sheet of paper left the office, she needed to tend to the special files—those that had been so dear to Winthrop's heart.

With a sense of purpose, she crossed the room to the cartons she'd filled herself. Large manila envelopes, along with a stack of typing paper the temp had failed to put away after mailing the real estate files, were on the desk next to them.

Abby stopped in front of a yellow carton. A small smile touched her lips as she looked fondly at the folders inside.

The babies, she thought, a rush of warmth suffusing her.

Winthrop's practice had been varied, but his favorite cases were the adoptions. He'd loved little children. Three cases in particular had been special to Winthrop: Shaw, Russell and Parker.

It was with that thought that she noticed the first folder wasn't the one she'd placed there yesterday. She was certain she'd left the Shaw file in front. She specifically remembered putting it there after instructing the temp to mail everything in the carton next to it.

Perplexed, she removed the box of stationery and mailing labels the woman had left on the box and searched through the remaining folders. The Parker and Russell files were there, but where was Shaw?

She went through the box again slowly, carefully checking each folder. Fifteen minutes later, she admitted defeat. The Shaw file was nowhere to be found. Deeply troubled, she picked up the Russell file.

Russell, Janice, she thought, reading the name on the folder tab. She frowned as she glanced through the papers. She'd never approved of Janice Russell's decision. It just wasn't right that the young man had never been told he was a father. He should know he had a child.

Abby reached for a mailing envelope.

Chapter One

Five Years Ago

As Tessa Russell entered the hospital, she was only vaguely aware of the bustling people, the bright lights, the faint odor of antiseptic.

She felt strange, disoriented, as though she were standing outside of herself, watching what she was doing from afar.

A part of her mind realized that she was in a state of semishock, and that it was imperative that she get a grip on herself in order to be prepared for what she was about to face.

Another part of her preferred to stay in her otherworld fog, where it was possible to postpone dealing with the harsh truths of reality.

The touch of a hand on her arm caused her to stop and look around at the attorney who had brought her here, the man who had been the cause of her life being suddenly turned upside down.

"Yes, Mr. Ames?" she said, her voice unsteady.

Winthrop Ames, Esq., was a short, round, balding man in his early sixties, who was dressed in a three-piece suit, complete with the old-fashioned touch of a watch chain. He had a surprisingly dynamic voice for someone of his small stature, and it must have served him well during his many years in the courtroom.

It was his eyes that Tessa sought, needing the gentleness and compassion evident there.

"Are you all right, Ms. Russell?" Winthrop asked.

"Yes. No." She shook her head. "I'm sorry. I'm not behaving very well. I know I must be strong, but it's just so much to comprehend." She drew a deep breath, then lifted her chin. "I'll be fine. You've been so kind, so caring, and I appreciate all you're doing."

"You're quite welcome."

She managed a small smile. "Attorneys, I'm afraid, have a reputation for being rather coldhearted and money-hungry, more often than not. You're a refreshing exception to the rule, Mr. Ames."

He chuckled. "That may be why I drive a ten-year-old car, and wear a suit every bit as ancient." His smile faded. "I deal in people, not cases, not clients given a number on a file folder, but human beings. I haven't been highly successful in the practice of law on a monetary level, Ms. Russell, but I sleep with an inner peace at night, and that's extremely important to me. I'm able to live with myself with a clear conscience."

Tessa nodded.

"Are you ready to go upstairs now, Ms. Russell?"

"Please, call me Tessa."

"Yes, all right, Tessa. Your sister is on the maternity floor, but is in a private room where her heart can be continually monitored, as well as a close watch kept on the condition of the baby."

"Janice," Tessa whispered, struggling against threatening tears. "It's been so many years since she ran away from the foster home where we were placed when our parents were killed. She was so unhappy and angry. Her world had been destroyed at twelve years old, and at fourteen, she disappeared during the night."

An errant tear slid down one cheek, and she dashed it away.

"For the past nine years, I didn't know if she was alive or dead, or what had happened to her," Tessa said. "And now? Dear God, she's about to give birth to a baby."

"Tessa," Winthrop said gently, "you must remember that Janice is extremely ill. The life-style she was caught up in, the drugs, alcohol... The toll on her heart has been devastating. The doctors have said that the chances of Janice surviving the birth of her child are very slim. She's aware of that fact, and she requested that I find you. You can be assured that she took excellent care of herself during her pregnancy for the sake of the child, and try to find solace in that."

"Yes. Yes, I will. Let's go upstairs, Mr. Ames. I want to see my sister."

Winthrop looked directly at her for long moment, then nodded.

* * *

Tessa stood next to the bed, gripping the top rung of the safety rail so tightly, her knuckles were white. Several machines nearby made strange beeping noises, and had wires trailing under the blanket covering Janice.

Tessa stared down at her sleeping sister, her heart aching and tears once again misting her eyes.

Janice was two years younger than Tessa, but appeared ten years older. She was pale and gaunt, with purple smudges beneath her closed eyes. Her short hair was tangled and dull, with no natural sheen.

She looked so small, so fragile, as though the slightest breeze could fling her into oblivion.

Janice was dying.

"Dear God," Tessa said, pressing the fingertips of one hand to her lips to stifle a sob.

She forced herself to shift her tormented gaze to the mound that was Janice's stomach pressing against the light green blanket.

A baby, Tessa thought. A miracle. Somehow, for the sake of her own sanity, she had to concentrate on the life, not the pending death, within her view.

Winthrop Ames had explained that Janice had first approached him to assist her with plans to place the baby for adoption. She'd refused to name the father.

As the months passed, Janice had changed her mind, deciding to keep the baby so she would have someone to love, someone to love her.

Winthrop had finally convinced Janice that as a single parent, she owed it to her baby to name a guardian in the event that something should happen to her, the child's mother.

He'd also persuaded her to identify the father in case a unique and life-threatening medical problem arose with the child. The biological father's blood or bone marrow might mean the difference between life and death. Janice had reluctantly agreed. Tessa Russell was to be the baby's legal guardian.

Oh, Janice, Tessa thought, *why didn't you come to me years ago?* Janice had told Winthrop that Tessa was living in Tucson, and she had even known the address and telephone number. She was too ashamed of how she'd lived her life, she'd told the attorney, to contact her older sister.

Tessa shook her head. She wouldn't have stood in judgment of Janice. She would have been overjoyed to have welcomed her into her life and home. But now it was too late. Too late.

Janice stirred and opened her eyes.

"Tessa?" she said, her voice weak.

"I'm here. Oh, Janice, I . . ." Tears choked off Tessa's words.

"Don't cry. Please, Tessa, there isn't time for tears, for sorrow. We have to think of the baby. Listen to me, please?"

"Yes, I'm listening. Don't tire yourself."

"I'm not important now. I know I'm dying, Tessa, but my baby is alive and healthy." She smiled. "It's a boy. They told me after one of my tests. A little boy."

"That's wonderful," Tessa said, managing to smile through her tears. "What would you like to name him?"

Janice's smile faded. "*You* decide on his name. You're going to be his mother." She paused and her eyes widened. "Oh, God, Tessa, you *will* take my baby, won't you? Please? Oh, please, Tessa?"

Tessa covered one of Janice's hands with her own. "Shh, calm down. You mustn't upset yourself like this. Of course I'll love him as my own, and raise him the very best I can." Tears spilled onto her cheeks. "I'm sorry, but this is so difficult. I've missed you, Janice, so very much."

"Forgive me for causing you such pain. That's all I can say... please forgive me, because there isn't time to explain how I felt during those years, how angry and confused I was. It doesn't matter now."

Tessa nodded as she swept the tears away.

"Tessa, you must promise me that you won't contact the baby's father. Mr. Ames convinced me to have his name on file in case of a medical emergency. If that occurs, God forbid, then... But otherwise, the father isn't to be told. Will you promise me that?"

"Why, Janice? You obviously feel very strongly about this, but why?"

Janice sighed wearily. "It was a fling, a party, nothing more. I was living in Las Vegas, and he came with friends to celebrate the opening of his own law practice in Tucson. All he thinks about is money. He's cold, hard and places money at the top of his list of importance. Oh, he's very handsome, and he's a fantastic lover, I'll give him that. *But the man has no soul.* Keep him away from my baby, Tessa. *Please.*"

"Don't excite yourself, Janice."

"Promise me!"

"Yes, yes, I promise."

"Thank you. Thank you. I knew you lived in Tucson, and I moved here to Phoenix when I discovered I was pregnant so I would feel closer to you. But I couldn't face you, I just couldn't." Her eyes drifted closed. "I'm so tired, so tired. I love you very much, Tessa."

"I love you, too, Janice," she whispered.

Tessa covered her face with her hands and wept softly.

Jason Robert Russell came into the world with a lusty wail and a fluffy cap of black hair. He weighed seven pounds, seven ounces, and was declared to be perfectly healthy. Tessa named him Jason as a male version of Janice, and Robert for his deceased grandfather, Janice and Tessa's father.

Janice Russell died peacefully in her sleep less than an hour after the birth.

Forty-eight hours later, following a memorial service for her sister, Tessa Russell took the precious baby home.

Chapter Two

The Present

Dominic Bonelli replaced the receiver of the telephone, then rotated his head back and forth in an attempt to loosen the tightened muscles in his neck and shoulders.

He'd been talking on the telephone for almost two hours in a tough negotiating session with the attorney representing the principals wanting to purchase the company that Dominic's client wished to sell.

Four additional clauses of the complicated contract had been ironed out, line by line, some even word by word.

There was a lot of work yet to do, Dominic knew, but the deal was steadily moving forward. The concessions he'd had to make had been few, and if things continued as they were, his client would be extremely pleased.

There was no if about it, he decided. The final contract would lean heavily in his client's favor. Dominic would have won the disputed issues of importance, and given in on only minor details. While the attorney for the buyer was crowing over Dominic's defeats, the seller would have everything Dominic had set out to gain.

He nodded in satisfaction. Each new deal he undertook was a challenge, with strategies to be planned after hours spent studying the facts down to the most minute detail. It was a game of sorts, that required knowing the opposition every bit as well as his own client.

His reputation in Tucson—in fact, across the state—for being a sharp, aggressive corporate attorney, who hammered away at contracts until they were letter-perfect, was growing. The ever-increasing number of clients coming through the door was evidence of his expertise.

Dominic Bonelli, attorney-at-law, was on his way to the top at only thirty-five years old. Nothing, and no one, would keep him from reaching his career goals.

A light tap on his office door brought him from his pleasant reverie, and he answered the summons with an automatic, "Come in."

A woman in her early fifties entered the large room. Gladys Weber was short, rather plump, wore her gray hair in a bun at the nape of her neck and had a smile always at the ready.

She looked, Dominic had once told her, like someone who should be home baking cookies for her grandchildren. Her grandkids, she'd retorted, ate store-bought cookies at her house. She was a top-notch administrative assistant, thank you very much, and Dominic would do well to remember that. His reply had been a grin.

"You'll have to speak up, Gladys," Dominic said as she stopped in front of his enormous desk. "My ear died."

"I don't doubt it. You were certainly on the phone a long time. I thought that little red light on my console was never going to blink off. Half the morning is gone." She deposited a stack of material in front of him. "Your mail, master, and the messages from everyone who tried to reach you for the past two hours." She paused. "I assume the negotiations are going well?"

"They are," he said with a decisive nod.

"Of course. Oh, there's an envelope in that stack marked personal that I didn't open. It's that legal-size one on the bottom. Are you taking calls yet?"

"No, give me about fifteen minutes to clear my head and go through this mail, then I'll be back on duty."

"Got it." She turned and briskly walked from the room, closing the door behind her as she left.

Gladys was a gem, Dominic mused, staring at the closed door. She'd agreed to work for him when he'd started his own practice over five years before, gambling on the fact that he wasn't going to fall flat on his face.

They'd weathered the early days, the ones that had been financially lean despite the nest egg he'd been putting aside for years while eagerly anticipating the opening of his own firm. Then they'd cheered together as the client list grew. There were now two paralegals under Gladys's command, who respected and sincerely liked her.

She was a prize, no doubt about it. She put up with his dark moods, his intensity, his perfectionism. She even took his eccentricities in stride, such as his directive that his office door was to remain closed at all times.

Dominic leaned back in the butter-soft leather chair, resting his head against the high back and staring at the ceiling.

The sense of privacy the closed door afforded him was important. It continually reaffirmed where he was now, compared to where he had come from.

He lifted his head to sweep his gaze over the spacious, expensively decorated office. The furniture was gleaming mahogany, the thick carpeting was chocolate brown. The color scheme was dark blue with varying shades of browns and tans, lightening to off-white.

A grouping of easy chairs surrounding a low, round table was on the far side of the room, and two chairs were placed in front of his desk. The mahogany filing cabinets along one wall had been custom-built.

The room was masculine and richly appointed. The exact message he wished to convey to those entering was that of command and wealth.

Dominic's glance fell on the pile of mail in front of him, and he forced himself to end his mental ramblings. Curiosity rose to the fore, and he pulled free the unopened envelope Gladys had spoken of.

There was no return address, he noted, nor was there a typed mailing label. The writing was wobbly, as though the person's hand had been shaking.

He slit the top of the envelope with a letter opener, and withdrew a manila file folder. The tab on the side read: Russell, Janice.

Pushing the remaining mail to one side, he placed the file in front of him, and flipped it open. Within moments, a deep frown knitted his eyebrows.

"What in the hell," he muttered, then read further.

Rising fury caused his heartbeat to quicken, and every muscle in his body to tighten. As he finished reading the last document, he smacked the papers with the palm of one hand, and lunged to his feet.

Moving from behind his desk, he began to pace the floor with heavy, anger-induced steps.

He'd never heard of Janice or Tessa Russell, nor had he had any contact with a Phoenix attorney named Winthrop Ames.

The documents were dated over five years ago. Janice Russell had met with Winthrop Ames to discuss placing her then-unborn child for adoption upon its birth. She later changed her mind, having decided to keep the child.

A copy of Janice's death certificate was in the file, along with a copy of a birth certificate for Jason Robert Russell. The birth certificate had *unknown* in the space allotted for naming the father.

But, Dominic fumed, still pacing the floor, a separate sheet of paper was a legal form naming Dominic Bonelli as the father of the child. Tessa Russell, the deceased mother's sister, was the guardian of Jason Robert Russell, and had taken him from the hospital to her Tucson home at an address given.

What was the game plan? If these people were intent on slapping him with a phony paternity suit for child support, why wait five years? It was really stupid, because with the sophisticated tests available now, he could prove in an instant that he wasn't the father. If someone was attempting to instigate a con, they should at least have a modicum of brains.

"Hell," Dominic said with a snort of disgust.

He should ignore the whole thing. It wasn't worth his valuable time and energy to even acknowledge the arrival of the file.

He stopped and narrowed his eyes as he stared at the folder on the desk.

No, by damn, he decided, he wasn't going to let Winthrop Ames and Tessa Russell off that easily. They would come to know that they'd made a big mistake by trying to pull a scam on him. He'd hit them with a lawsuit that would have them running for cover.

Moving closer to the desk, Dominic pressed the button on the intercom.

"Gladys, find out everything you can on a Phoenix attorney named Winthrop Ames and report back to me right away."

"Roger. You're welcome."

"Thank you," he muttered.

He sat down in his chair and began to sort through the remaining mail, instantly realizing he was too furious to concentrate. He drummed the fingers of one hand impatiently on the top of the desk as he waited for the information from Gladys.

The intercom buzzed and he hit the button with more force than necessary.

"Yes?" he said.

"Winthrop Ames," Gladys said, "passed away about two weeks ago. He had no partners, and his practice is in the process of being disbanded."

"Thank you," Dominic said absently, his mind racing.

He sank back in the chair, laced his hands behind his head and glowered at the ceiling.

Interesting, he mused, *and very strange.* Winthrop Ames was out of the picture, leaving the spotlight on Tessa Russell. How had she gotten her hands on that folder?

He nodded.

Money. She'd approached whoever was shutting down Ames's practice and bought the damn file. Fine. He'd slap a suit on the seller, too. Tessa Russell had then doctored the documents, either alone or with the help of the seller, to include the one naming him as the father of Janice Russell's child. Clever to a point, but ridiculous considering present-day DNA tests.

Tessa Russell was going to regret having put her nasty little scheme in motion.

He looked at his appointment calendar, then pressed the intercom button again.

"Gladys, I'm going to keep my lunch date with Baxter because he's only down from Flagstaff for the day, but please reschedule my afternoon appointments. I'll be out of the office."

"Oh?"

"Don't get nosy."

"I'm not nosy, I'm efficient. Will I be able to reach you anywhere this afternoon?"

"No. I'll call in for my messages, or swing back by here, but I don't know what time."

"What if there's an emergency or..."

"Goodbye, Gladys."

* * *

It was after two o'clock before Dominic was able to end the luncheon appointment with Mr. Baxter. The Flagstaff client was retired, his time was his own and he seemed to derive a great deal of pleasure from going over every detail of the various buying-and-selling of properties that Dominic was handling for him.

At last free, Dominic consulted a city map, then drove out of the restaurant parking lot. The address given in the file for Tessa Russell was on the east side of town by the Rincon Mountains. He had to cross the city with its bumper-to-bumper traffic, and the going was slow.

Great, he thought as he stopped at yet another red light. He was getting a stress headache. He'd better chill out, as one of his nephews would say. Tensing with anger to the point of subjecting himself to painfully throbbing temples wasn't going to make the traffic move any faster so that he could confront Tessa Russell.

Taking a deep breath, he let it out slowly, then forced himself to shift mental gears.

The weather. That was an innocuous subject. September was a perfect time of year in Tucson. The daily rains of the summer monsoons were over, and the desert was a lush expanse of vivid colors displayed by scrub grass and wildflowers. The days were warm and the nights were cool enough for retrieving blankets from the closet shelf.

The three mountain ranges edging the city, the Santa Catalinas, the Rincons and the Tucsons, stood out in sharp relief against a brilliant blue sky dotted with fluffy white clouds.

"Very nice day," he said aloud, then rolled his eyes heavenward.

Finally, the traffic began to thin as Dominic drove farther away from town. He pressed harder on the gas pedal of his silver BMW, relishing the feel of the powerful vehicle responding to his command.

The paved road soon turned to dirt, creating a cloud of dust that left a coating on Dominic's sparkling clean car. His frame of mind *definitely* did not improve.

Consulting the map he'd placed next to him on the plush seat, he at last turned onto a side road, immediately slowing as he hit a pothole.

"Hell," he said as he saw that the road had more ruts than smooth surfaces.

The narrow road curved and Dominic drove on, seeing a house that was situated, in his opinion, in the middle of nowhere. The majestic Rincon Mountains were in the distance, desert stretched as far as the eye could see and there was the house, appearing as though it had been plunked down there as an afterthought.

He pressed on the brake at the end of a driveway leading to the structure, and checked the number on the mailbox mounted on a post.

Nodding as he saw that the number matched the one shown in the file, he folded his arms on top of the steering wheel and scrutinized the house, which was about two hundred yards away.

It was an old, two-story wooden house badly in need of paint. A porch stretched across the entire front, displaying a bench swing suspended by chains and several white wicker chairs.

Mounted just above the steps was a multicolored sign that read: Rainbow's End Day-Care Center. A chain-link fence was on one side of the house, creating an area where children were playing on a variety of equipment.

So, Dominic mused, Tessa Russell ran a baby-sitting service in a house that looked as though it might be blown away by a gust of wind. Well, it wasn't going to be *his* money that would spruce up this dump.

"Nice try, Tessa," he said under his breath. "But no cigar."

He drove to the front of the house, the driveway even bumpier than the road leading to it. He parked the vehicle. Grabbing his briefcase, he left the car and went up the rickety steps. Hesitating a moment, he decided it wasn't necessary to knock on the door of a business. He entered the house, a tinkling bell above the door announcing his arrival.

Sweeping his gaze quickly over the room, he mentally cataloged the worn carpeting and furniture. Against one wall was a wooden creation of connected, open square boxes, each with a name printed on cardboard above the opening. Another unit had shelves with toys and books. A neat stack of small throw rugs was in a corner beyond a flight of stairs that no doubt led to the second floor.

Everything was extremely shabby, he thought. The inside needed painting as badly as the exterior, but at least it was clean.

He sniffed the air, finally identifying the faint aroma as cinnamon.

"I'll be right with you," a woman called from somewhere in the distance.

Dominic buttoned his suit coat, straightened his shoulders and waited.

Tessa slid the last snickerdoodle off the cookie sheet, then quickly removed the hot-pad mitts. Straightening the waistband of her royal blue T-shirt over her faded jeans, she blew a puff of air upward in a futile attempt to create a semblance of order to her naturally curly bangs. She hurried from the kitchen to greet whoever had entered the house.

As she went into the living room, she slowed her step to enable herself to take a quick mental inventory of the man standing by the front door.

Tall, dark and handsome, she thought. Whoever had invented the cliché must have had someone like this in mind. He appeared to be about six feet tall, was around thirty-five and drop-dead gorgeous.

Hair...dark as night. Eyes...ebony pools surrounded by long eyelashes a woman would die for. Physique...perfectly proportioned, with wide shoulders, narrow hips, long legs, all of which were displayed to perfection in what was obviously a custom-tailored suit. Features...strong and rugged, extremely masculine rather than pretty-boy smooth. Tanned, but then, maybe not. He looked Italian, or perhaps Greek, so the bronzed glow of his skin was one of nature's gifts of his heritage.

And, darn it, he was carrying a briefcase. Mr. Scrumptious was a salesman, albeit a very impressive-looking one. So, okay, she was now in her polite, but firm, no-I-don't-want-to-buy-any-insurance mode.

She stopped ten feet in front of him.

"Hello," she said pleasantly. "I'm Tessa Russell, the owner of Rainbow's End. How may I help you?"

Dominic narrowed his eyes slightly.

So, this was the con artist, he mused. She certainly didn't look the part. She was tall, slender but not skinny, had short, curly, strawberry-blond hair, and the biggest brown eyes he'd ever seen.

She was close to thirty, he supposed, but appeared younger in a refreshing, no-makeup way. She could be a wholesome-model candidate for a box of cornflakes.

But he knew better. He had her number. While he wasn't a trial lawyer, he'd spent enough time in the courthouse to be aware that the less-than-savory came in all shapes, sizes and ages. Tessa Russell was a crook-in-training.

"Sir?" Tessa said, frowning slightly.

Dominic brought his thoughts to an abrupt halt and looked directly into Tessa's eyes.

"I'm here," he said, his voice ominously low, "in response to the information I received from you in the mail today, Ms. Russell."

Tessa's frown deepened. "I'm afraid I don't understand. I mailed you something? An insurance payment or... Excuse me, because I don't mean to be rude, but who are you?"

A pulse began to beat wildly in Dominic's temple as his anger soared once again.

"Dominic Bonelli."

The knot that tightened instantly in Tessa's stomach was so painful, she instinctively wrapped her hands around her elbows in a protective gesture. She could actually feel the color draining from her face.

Dear God, no! her mind screamed. She used to have a bone-chilling fear that Dominic Bonelli would somehow learn of his son's existence, and arrive like an evil demon in the night to snatch her Jason.

But as the years passed, she'd calmed that terrifying thought until it was finally gone, flung into oblivion for all time.

And now? He was there, standing no more than a few feet away. He was big, strong, and because he was an attorney, he was also very powerful in the arena of the law.

Please. No. This couldn't be happening. But it was. *Dominic Bonelli was here.*

"My, my, Ms. Russell," Dominic said, sarcasm ringing in his voice, "you seem shaken. Surely you expected me to respond to what you sent me."

Tessa reached deep within herself for all the emotional strength she possessed. Her life was at stake.

"I'm not upset in the least, Mr. Bonelli," she said, lifting her chin. "I didn't have time for lunch today, and felt light-headed for a moment." She attempted a smile that failed to materialize. "Now then, let's clear up this matter, shall we? I'm very busy. I did *not* send anything to you through the mail. I don't even know you."

"Nor do I know you, or your deceased sister, Janice."

Tessa's eyes widened. "Janice?"

"Do you have an office where we can discuss this?"

"Yes, I have an office, but there's nothing to discuss. My sister died over five years ago. I can't imagine what you received pertaining to her, but it's obviously a mistake."

"Oh, yes, indeed," he said, nodding. She'd chosen the wrong man to attempt to fleece. Ms. Russell was in a great deal of trouble. "It was a very big mistake on your part."

"You're talking in riddles, and I've had quite enough of your veiled threats. I'd like you to leave my home immediately."

"You live here?" he said, glancing around. "How quaint."

"Goodbye, Mr. Bonelli."

"I think not. You've apparently gotten cold feet now that we're face-to-face, but I have every intention of pursuing the matter and filing charges against you."

"For what?" she said, nearly shrieking.

"Try extortion, libel, defamation of character, mental duress, for starters."

"You're out of your mind."

"*You* were, to think you could pull this off. I have in my possession the file you mailed me. You remember the file, don't you? It's the one with the phony document naming me as the father of Janice Russell's child, the boy you became legal guardian of when your sister died."

"That's impossible. Winthrop Ames would never have—"

"Winthrop Ames has been dead for two weeks. You managed to get your hands on the file, added the form naming me as the baby's father and set your plan in motion. I'm curious... Why me? Did you simply turn to the page in the telephone directory listing attorneys and pick one, figuring lawyers made enough money to serve your purpose?"

"I repeat, Mr. Bonelli," Tessa said, her voice trembling, "you're out of your mind. Yes, my sister died the day her baby was born. And, yes, I'm his guardian, which is not a fact anyone knows besides myself, Mr. Ames and the court. The baby's birth certificate states that the father is unknown.

"I wasn't aware that Mr. Ames had passed away. I have no idea who sent you that file, or why they added the document you're speaking of. What I *do* know is that it wasn't me."

Doubt flickered through Dominic's mind. Had he acted too hastily? Had the mailing of the file been step one, with contact to follow from whoever was behind the scam? Was it possible that Tessa Russell was innocent of any wrongdoing?

"You've spoken of pressing charges against me," Tessa said coolly. "Well, I'm in a position to file a complaint against you, sir. This is an invasion of my privacy, and is placing the mental well-being of a child at risk. I've chosen to allow him to believe that I'm his natural mother until he is of an age to comprehend the truth. He will be told, at some point in the future, in accordance with my sister's wishes, that his father is unknown.

"Someone, Mr. Bonelli, is trying to extort money from you. Quite frankly, that is *your* problem. However, if one word of my true relationship to the child in question becomes public knowledge while you're dealing with this situation, I'll sue you. Count on it."

"Nicely said, Ms. Russell, but I have further questions to ask you. I want to know the names of everyone who worked in Winthrop Ames's office. I want to know if Ames or your sister ever referred to me in any manner. I want to know—"

"I have nothing more to say to you," Tessa interrupted. "Leave my home. Now."

Dominic studied her pale face for a long moment before speaking.

"All right," he said finally. "I'll leave. If you're as innocent as you claim, I'll be contacted by the culprit very soon, I imagine. If that occurs, I'll inform you of that fact, and apologize for distressing you. I will also guarantee you of my silence regarding your relationship with the child by requesting that the complaint I register against whoever is behind this is heard in judge's chambers."

"Fine."

"However, if I am *not* contacted, I'll be back, Ms. Russell. The cast of players will have narrowed down to one. You. Only you."

"Goodbye, Mr. Bonelli."

Dominic turned and started toward the door.

Go, Tessa mentally pleaded. Go, and never come back. Three more steps, and Dominic Bonelli would be out of her life. Jason would be safe again, with her, where he belonged. Three more steps. Two. One. Just one more.

As Dominic reached for the knob, the door burst open and a small boy ran in, carrying a paper cup he was covering with one hand.

"Mom," he yelled. "Mommy, guess what? I caught a lizard. It's here in this cup. Wanna see? He's cool, Mom. Can I keep him?"

Dominic stared at the boy, seeing his black hair, dark eyes with long lashes, the tawny hue of his skin.

Dear Lord, he thought, he looked exactly like himself in the photos his mother kept in the family album. The boy looked like his nephews had, too, at around five years old. He looked like a Bonelli.

No, damn it. It was impossible. The whole situation was so infuriating, he wasn't thinking clearly. He was allowing his imagination to run away with him.

Perhaps Janice Russell's lover had looked like him. It was a strange coincidence, nothing more. But he'd never heard of Janice Russell, and was not the father of her child. *This boy was not his son.*

"Hi," the boy said, turning to Dominic. "Wanna see my lizard?"

"Another time, perhaps," Dominic said. "Aren't you going to introduce me to this young man, Ms. Russell?"

"Mr. Bonelli," Tessa said, her voice now strong and steady, "this is Jason Robert Russell. *My son.*"

Chapter Three

The remainder of the workday seemed endless to Tessa. She performed by rote, having the strange sensation of being detached from herself as she watched her interaction with the children.

Each time she replayed in her mind the scene with Dominic Bonelli, she was consumed by chilling fear. She wanted to snatch up Jason and run as far away as possible as quickly as she could.

After Dominic had left the house, she'd admonished herself for having admitted that she was Jason's legal guardian due to Janice's death. And by telling Dominic that Jason was not aware of the truth, she'd given the threatening man the power to make her dance to his tune in exchange for his silence.

Many years before, she'd vowed to never again relinquish control of her life. After the nightmare of losing her parents, and being at the mercy of the foster-home system, she was determined that no one would ever dictate to her again.

She'd been furious with herself for so readily admitting her true relationship with Jason. But as the hours passed, she'd realized that she'd had no choice.

Dominic Bonelli had the file from Winthrop Ames's office. If Dominic chose to verify the authenticity of the death and birth certificates, it would be a simple task to accomplish. To deny that Janice had been Jason's natural mother would have been foolish.

She'd taken the only viable stand, she'd finally decided. It was true that she had no idea who had mailed the file to Dominic. But she had to adamantly maintain that the document naming Dominic as Jason's father was false. It was a mistake, or hoax, or an attempt to extort money from Dominic. Whatever the reason, she knew nothing about it.

Dominic Bonelli must never know that Jason was his son.

During the tedious afternoon, both of Tessa's employees, Patty and Emma, had asked her if she was all right. She'd pleaded a headache, managed to smile and continued with her duties.

Jason had been reluctantly convinced that the tiny lizard would be happier if allowed to go free to scamper along the desert floor.

Each time Tessa had looked at Jason, her heart quickened in terror. Dominic Bonelli possessed the power to take her son away from her. The court would lean heavily in favor of custody being given to a natural father over an aunt named as legal guardian.

Oh, God, no! her mind had hammered over and over. Jason was *her* baby, *her* beloved son.

* * *

At nine o'clock that night, Tessa stood next to Jason's bed, watching him sleep. In the glow of the night-light, she could see him clearly. His dark hair was a silky tumble, his long lashes lay like delicate fans on his cheeks.

He was so beautiful, she mused. He was a healthy, happy little boy. From the moment he'd been placed in her arms, she'd been filled with a love of such intensity, it was nearly painful.

When she'd left the foster home, she'd had a dream. She would someday have her own business. *She* would be in charge, in control. *She* would command her destiny.

The arrival of Jason into her life had been her call to action. She'd saved every penny she could during the years she'd worked as a waitress, and taken endless courses in business management, accounting, business law and taxes.

Her sudden and unexpected role as a single mother had given her the solution to the yet unanswered question of what type of business she wished to have. A day-care center. It was perfect. She could raise Jason herself, and still provide for their welfare.

For five blissful years, everything had been wonderful. There was very little money left over for extras after paying expenses, but Rainbow's End was holding its own. She even had a waiting list of those wishing to bring their children here, despite the location's being off the beaten track.

She was proud of what she'd accomplished in the past five years. And each morning as parents dropped off their children, she still felt a rush of joy that she didn't have to leave Jason.

They'd been a team, mother and son, since he was born. Laughter had echoed within the walls of the old house. Jason had cut his first tooth here, taken his first steps, spoken his first words. It was their home, where Tessa could close the door against the world. It was their safe haven.

Until now.

Until Dominic Bonelli had entered that house and threatened all that Tessa held dear. He had the power to shatter her existence.

With a ragged sigh that held a hint of a sob, she leaned over and kissed Jason gently on the forehead. She left the bedroom and went into the living room.

As she sank onto the worn sofa, crushing exhaustion overcame her. Tears filled her eyes and she lacked the energy to struggle against them.

What would happen next? she wondered frantically. She'd managed to instill doubt in Dominic's mind, but even though he'd backed off, he was not convinced that she was blameless.

Who had mailed him the file? And why? The culprit wasn't after him for child support. Did someone actually believe in these modern times that a prominent attorney would feel his reputation was at risk because he'd fathered a child out of wedlock? That was nonsense. Whoever had mailed the file was not in touch with reality. Dominic would deny that he was Jason's father, Tessa would concur and the extortionist would be left high and dry.

But if that person came to his senses and didn't contact Dominic further, the lawyer would come back to Rainbow's End. He wouldn't view the situation as a potential blackmailer having second thoughts. Oh, no, he'd made it clear that if he didn't hear from another source, then the nasty scheme had been Tessa's brainstorm.

And he would be back.

"Dear God," she whispered as a chill swept through her.

Shaking her head in despair, she gave way to the tears, and cried.

An entire week passed with no word from Dominic Bonelli. As each day went by, Tessa's hope that she would never hear from him again grew stronger.

A part of her mind registered the urge to look up his telephone number in the directory and call him, to get some kind of emotional closure of the situation. She needed something, anything, to reassure herself that Dominic was truly no longer a threat to her and Jason.

Another section of her brain refused to allow her to contact Dominic. Clichés such as *No news is good news* and *Let sleeping dogs lie* flickered in her mind, and she finally dismissed the idea of calling him.

She *did,* however, dial Information to ask for the number of Winthrop Ames's office. The kind and compassionate attorney had passed away, but perhaps there was someone still in his office who might have a clue as to how the confidential file had come to be mailed to Dominic. The operator informed her that the number was no longer in service.

Another day of blessed silence, Tessa thought as she waved goodbye to the last child leaving Rainbow's End. Another day without hearing from Dominic Bonelli.

"I'm off," Patty said, bringing Tessa from her thoughts.

"Me, too," Emma said. "It was a typical exhausting Monday. The kids are so rambunctious after the weekend. I swear, they must spend every Saturday and Sunday eating nothing but sweets. They're so wired on Mondays, like bouncing kangaroos."

Tessa laughed. "That's a perfect description of our little darlings on a Monday."

"Tomorrow will be better," Patty said. "Good night, Tessa. Have a nice evening, and go to bed early. You looked so tired all of last week, and the weekend didn't erase those dark smudges under your eyes."

"Yes, I'll go to bed early," Tessa said, smiling.

"I should hope so," Emma said.

Tessa stood at the door and watched as the two women went to their cars.

They were wonderful, she thought, both of them. They were in their early fifties and their grandchildren lived in other states. Rainbow's End gave them a chance to be with children, as well as the opportunity to earn some money. She was fortunate to have them.

"Mom?"

Tessa looked down at a frowning Jason. "Yes, sir?" she said, smiling at him. "You rang?"

"I'm hungry."

She ruffled his silky black hair. "You're always hungry. This time, your tummy is on schedule. I'll fix dinner pronto, Tonto. You can set the table."

"Can I make airplane napkins?"

"Sure. I think it's very classy to have a napkin by my plate that's folded into an airplane."

"Okay," he said, then ran toward the kitchen.

The upstairs of the house had three bedrooms and a bathroom. Tessa had furnished one of the bedrooms as a living room, with a sofa, a small easy chair, coffee and end tables. A television was set on top of a low bookcase.

It was in that cozy room that she and Jason spent their evenings. After they ate dinner, she would prepare fresh juice and snacks for the children for the next day, then she and Jason would "go home." The telephone was wired to ring in the kitchen, as well as the living room above.

Shortly after eight o'clock, Tessa finished reading Jason his nightly story, then kissed him on the forehead. He pulled the covers to beneath his chin, and wiggled into a comfortable position in his bed.

"Good night, good night," Tessa said. "Don't let the bedbugs bite."

Jason giggled.

"I love you, Jason Robert," she said.

"I love you, too, Mom," he said. "Whole bunches."

Tessa kissed him once more, this time on the tip of his nose, then left the room, knowing he would be asleep within minutes.

Jason went at full speed all day, she mused, going back into the living room. He was a bundle of energy, a healthy, joyful little boy. He *was* always hungry, it seemed, and was growing like a weed. He was probably going to be a tall man like his father.

She stopped statue-still by the sofa.

Dear heaven, where had that thought come from? She wanted no connection between Jason and Dominic, not even in her mind.

She sank onto one of the rather lumpy cushions of the sofa.

It was going to be more difficult now that she'd actually seen Dominic Bonelli. Ever since Jason was born, the man who had fathered him had been nothing more than a shadowy figure with no substance or form. He'd had a name, that was all.

But now? The resemblance between Jason and Dominic was uncanny. Jason was a miniature Dominic, with no visible trace of Janice.

Why hadn't Dominic seen the mirror image of himself when he'd looked at Jason? She'd been terrified when Jason had come dashing in the door the day Dominic had been here. He'd insisted on being introduced to the little boy, but there had been no shock, or wonder, in his expression when he'd said hello to Jason.

She should count her blessings that Dominic hadn't seen the carbon copy of himself in Jason. She was positive that if Emma or Patty had seen the pair together, they would have had questions as to the relationship between the two.

Had Dominic been too angry to really see the evidence before his eyes? Yes, that was a distinct possibility. That, along with the fact that he had no recollection of knowing Janice, had probably caused him to dismiss Jason out of hand.

On another, calmer occasion, Dominic might take a closer look at Jason and *see* the small duplicate of himself.

Hopefully, she would never hear from Dominic Bonelli again. But if she did, she must make very certain that he didn't come in contact with Jason.

The shrill ringing of the telephone caused Tessa to jerk in surprise at the sudden noise in the quiet room. She picked up the receiver.

"Hello?"

"Ms. Russell? This is Dominic Bonelli."

Dear heaven, Tessa's mind screamed. *I've conjured him up by thinking about him.* No, that was ridiculous. She had to get a grip on herself. *Now.*

"Ms. Russell?"

"Yes, I'm here."

"I waited until this hour to call in hopes that the boy would be asleep so we could speak privately."

"Oh?"

"I've not been contacted by anyone regarding the file, Ms. Russell. I decided to allow one week to go by before taking further action. Is the boy in bed?"

"Yes."

"Fine. I'm leaving here now, and should arrive at your house in half an hour, or so."

"Now wait just a minute. This is my home. You have no right to simply announce that you're coming here."

"I have every right. Thirty minutes. You and I are going to have what I predict will be a very interesting and revealing chat."

"No, I—" Tessa stopped speaking when she realized she was speaking to the dial tone.

She slammed the receiver into place and got to her feet, only to sink back onto the sofa an instant later as her trembling legs refused to support her.

Thirty minutes, her mind echoed. She had half an hour to prepare for the arrival of the man who held the power to destroy her life.

Chapter Four

Tessa entertained the idea of changing her clothes, then rejected the thought. Jeans, a shell-pink knit top and tennis shoes were just fine. She didn't wish to impress Dominic Bonelli, she just wanted him out of her life.

Should she offer him refreshments? she wondered, pacing restlessly around the living room. No, forget it. This was definitely not a social call.

She'd prefer to meet with him in her small office off of the kitchen downstairs, rather than have him upstairs in her home. But she had no choice but to bring him up; she wouldn't be comfortable leaving Jason all alone in their living quarters. He rarely awakened once he was asleep for the night, but when he had, she'd always been there for him.

She was, Tessa suddenly realized, bouncing back and forth between the emotions of fear and anger.

She was terrified of Dominic Bonelli and what he might do if he realized that Jason was indeed his son.

And she was mad as blue blazes at Dominic's overbearing attitude, the way he snapped orders, and his threats of filing charges against her. He was brash, arrogant and extremely rude.

Dominic was obviously quite accustomed to being in control and command, having things done his way with no questions asked.

Well, she had news for Mr. Bonelli. She wasn't going to bow three times, then jump to carry out his directives. She'd stand firm. She'd continue to state that she'd never heard of him, she'd maintain that the form in the file naming him as Jason's father was some kind of error that she knew nothing about and that there was nothing for him to gain by harassing her further.

Fine, she thought, walking to the window. She was no longer shifting between fear and anger. She was solidly set on *mad as hell,* which would serve her very well.

Brushing back the curtains, she saw the bobbing headlights of an approaching vehicle. It probably irritated the mighty Dominic Bonelli no end to have his fancy car jarred and covered in dust on the road leading to Rainbow's End. Good. It served him right for insisting on coming here again and invading her privacy.

Tessa waited until the car turned into the driveway, then went downstairs. There was a night-light in the front room, and she decided not to turn on any other lights. It might be taken as a welcoming gesture.

The bell rang, Tessa counted slowly to thirty, then opened the door.

"Come in," she said coolly, unlatching the screen.

Suit, tie and briefcase, she thought as Dominic moved past her. Did he ever remove his attorney uniform? He probably slept in it.

"Ms. Russell," Dominic said with a slight nod.

"This way," she said, not acknowledging his brisk greeting.

When she crossed the room and started up the stairs with Dominic following her, she was suddenly aware that he was getting an eyeful of her bottom encased as they were in her snug jeans.

So what? He wasn't a man, he was a menace. That he was one of the best-looking men she'd ever encountered meant nothing to her, and she couldn't care less what he thought of her as a woman.

She wouldn't be remotely close to being his type, anyway. He no doubt dated classy, sophisticated women from the high-society, wealthy set.

Unless he was married.

Tessa stumbled slightly at the unexpected thought. It had never occurred to her that Dominic Bonelli might be married. If he was, surely his wife wouldn't be overjoyed at learning he'd fathered a child five years ago, and now intended to gain custody of his son and bring him into their family.

Fantastic, she thought, renewed hope surging through her. She'd stay on alert to await just the right moment to hit him with the ramifications of taking Jason from her. Perhaps he was still so angry, he hadn't projected any of his actions into the future.

With any luck at all, though, things wouldn't get that far. She had to stay calm and cool, and keep repeating like a broken record that the form in the file was erroneous.

When they entered the living room, Tessa waved one hand toward the easy chair, knowing it was lumpier than the sofa.

"Have a seat," she said, settling onto the sofa.

Dominic sat down, resisted the urge to immediately stand up again as he felt a spring poke his backside, then leaned his briefcase against the side of the chair. He swept his gaze around the small room.

It was like the lower level of the house, he thought. Clean, but shabby.

"Please get on with whatever it is you came here to say," Tessa told him, looking somewhere over his right shoulder. "I get up very early in the morning, so I don't stay up late at night. Therefore, I'd appreciate your speaking your piece and leaving as quickly as possible."

Well, well, Dominic thought, surprised that he had to suppress a smile. Ms. Russell was in a feisty mood tonight. There was a determined lift to her chin, and a flush on her cheeks. She really was quite attractive, and certainly filled out tight jeans nicely. She was not his type, of course, but she was definitely capable of turning heads when she entered a room.

What would she look like in a stunning evening dress, instead of faded jeans? Even more, what would she look like wearing nothing at all?

Lord, Bonelli, he admonished himself, knock it off. Tessa Russell wasn't a woman, she was a nuisance.

"Mr. Bonelli?"

"You know why I'm here," he said, pulling his thoughts back to the moment at hand. "I told you when we first met that if I wasn't contacted by anyone else, the cast of players would be narrowed down to you. That's precisely what has happened. I presume your intentions were to extort a large sum of money from me?''

"This is the last time I'm going to say this, Mr. Bonelli. I have no idea how that file came to be in your possession, nor do I know who prepared the false document naming you as my son's father. I want nothing from you, except for you to leave me alone. Jason is mine, he has nothing whatsoever to do with you, and that is that.

"I'm willing to sign an affidavit stating that I have not contacted you in the past, nor will I ever contact you in regard to Jason, in exchange for a document from you guaranteeing your silence about my being Jason's aunt, rather than his natural mother. That should cover everything quite nicely.''

"No, I don't believe it will.''

Tessa got to her feet. "What on earth is the matter with you? Have you considered the damage you could do to others by pursuing this nonsense? Have you thought of anyone other than yourself?''

This was it, she decided. This was the time to play her ace.

"What about your own family, your wife and children?'' she went on. "If Jason was your son—which he isn't—do you think your wife would be thrilled to make a home for him if you gained custody?

"So, fine, Jason isn't yours. But what kind of distress do you think it would cause your wife if she discovered there was a document stating that he was? Have you thought further than your own anger? Don't you care about the people you love?''

"I have never been married.''

Oh, hell, Tessa thought, sinking back onto the sofa.

Dominic studied her face for a long moment as he sifted and sorted the data in his mind.

"Perhaps you're right, Ms. Russell," he finally said slowly. "I may not be thinking past my anger. If you wanted money, this would be the time to demand it. You've either gotten cold feet, or you're actually as innocent as you profess to be."

"Cold feet?" Tessa said, her voice rising. "I really resent—"

"Yes, all right," he interrupted, raising both hands. "I'll give consideration to the affidavits you proposed, and contact you in the next few days." He got to his feet. "I . . ."

Dominic stopped speaking and frowned as the telephone suddenly began to make strange noises, sounding almost like a quacking duck. Tessa was paying absolutely no attention to the intrusive noise.

"What's wrong with your telephone?" he said.

"My phone?" she said, momentarily confused by his abrupt change of subject. "I don't even hear that nonsense anymore. Sometimes it just squeaks, squawks, whatever you want to call it."

"It quacks," he said, his frown deepening. "Have you told the telephone company about this?"

"Yes." She shrugged. "They can't figure it out, either. It doesn't do it very often, and there's no pattern to it, so I just ignore it. Jason loves it. He says it's E.T. trying to phone *our* home."

Dominic crossed the room and picked up the receiver, giving it a sharp shake. It quacked.

"Ridiculous," he said. "Hold down the button on the base to cut off the dial tone." He began to unscrew the mouthpiece. "The button?"

Tessa got to her feet and moved around him to do as instructed.

He certainly was pushy, she thought, considering the fact it was *her* telephone that was "quacking," to quote Mr. Bonelli. Well, at least his mind had shifted to something other than the reason for his being here.

"Hold this," he said, extending the mouthpiece toward her.

As Tessa took the round piece of plastic from Dominic, their hands brushed in a light, fleeting motion that seemed to her to encompass minutes instead of seconds. A flutter of heat skittered along her spine.

She snapped her head up to look at him, only to find that he was staring directly at her. As though they'd both been delivered the message at the same time that they were standing so close together their bodies were nearly touching, they each took a step backward.

Dominic cleared his throat, directed his attention to the telephone, and began to fiddle with some wires. A few minutes later, he retrieved the mouthpiece from Tessa's outstretched palm, and twisted it into place. He returned the receiver to the base of the telephone.

"That should take care of it," he said. "There was a loose connection inside. I would have thought a telephone company repairman would have seen it easily enough. Well, it's fixed now."

He started across the room to where he'd left his briefcase.

The telephone quacked.

A bubble of laughter escaped from Tessa's lips.

Dominic spun around and glowered at the telephone, glaring at Tessa for good measure.

"If I were you," she said, unable to curb her smile, "I wouldn't moonlight as a telephone repairman."

"Yes, well," he said, then ran a restless hand down his tie. "Forget it. Let's get back to the subject at hand, shall we?"

Tessa's smile instantly disappeared.

"I may never get to the bottom of *who* did this," Dominic said, "or *why* they did it. My time is too valuable to devote much more energy to the situation. It's probably best to put it to rest."

Tessa's heart began to pound and she had the near-hysterical urge to let out a loud cheer. This nightmare was almost over!

"Mommy?"

Tessa jumped to her feet at the sound of Jason's voice.

Dear heaven, no. Not again. Jason had entered the house just as Dominic was leaving the first time. Now it was happening again. *Oh, Jason, why did you wake up?*

"Mommy, I heard yelling."

"I'm sorry, sweetheart," she said, hurrying to him. "We didn't mean to disturb you. Let's get you tucked back into bed."

"Wait," Dominic said, his voice ringing with tension.

Tessa turned to look at him, and saw to her horror that he was staring intently at Jason.

My God, Dominic thought, this child had been fathered by a Bonelli. Jason Russell had a slight dip on the very top of his right ear that every Bonelli had had for generations. It was not that noticeable, and was easily covered by hair, but he could see it now in Jason's tousled state.

Tessa glared at Dominic, then ushered Jason from the room. After seeing him back into bed, she returned to the living room.

"I'll walk you to the front door, Mr. Bonelli," she said.

"No, I . . ." He dragged one hand through his hair. "This changes everything."

"What do you mean?"

"The boy's right ear, Ms. Russell. He has a slight dip on the top."

"So?"

"So, every Bonelli for generations has had that dip. As each of my nieces and nephews were born, we all said we could pick them out through the nursery window by looking at their right ear, no matter how many Italian babies might be on display."

"But . . ."

Dominic swept back the thick hair over his right ear. A chill coursed through Tessa as she saw the tiny dip that was exactly like Jason's. Dominic finger-combed his hair back into place.

"I rest my case," he said. "That boy is a Bonelli."

"That boy has a name," Tessa said, her voice quivering. "He's a living, breathing child. You spit out the word 'boy' as if it's distasteful to you. He is Jason Robert Russell." She fought against threatening tears. "*He is my son.* I swear to God that if you attempt to take him away from me, I'll fight you with every breath in my body."

"Take him away from you? Attempt to gain legal custody of him? Believe me, that is the last thing I'd do. You were right in saying that attention needs to be paid to the ramifications of this situation, the lives that could be irrevocably damaged." He paused. "Do you know where the boy...where Jason...was conceived?''

"I don't see what that has to do—"

"Where?" Dominic snapped.

"Las Vegas," she retorted.

"Damn it," he said, staring up at the ceiling. "Over five years ago in Las Vegas. It fits. Damn it, it fits." He looked at Tessa again. "Silence, Ms. Russell, is the word here. You and I are going to reach an agreement of absolute silence regarding *your* son's existence."

"You're confusing me," she said, shaking her head. "You're going on and on, and I don't understand."

"It's painfully clear. A little more than five years ago, I finally opened my own law firm. For the first time in my life, the very first, I decided to celebrate and have some fun. Well, there's obviously going to be a higher price to pay than just the tab I picked up for all of us."

"All of who?" she said, throwing up her hands in a gesture of frustration. "You're talking in riddles."

"Jason was conceived in Las Vegas during a wild and undisciplined celebration. He is, without a doubt, a Bonelli. Jason's father is a married man with children, and this would be extremely destructive to his marriage."

"But you said you've never been married."

"Not me," he said, splaying out one hand on his chest. "I would never behave in such an irresponsible manner. Oh, no, Ms. Russell, not me. Jason's father is one of my four brothers."

Chapter Five

Tessa opened her mouth, then immediately snapped it closed.

Without realizing she had done it, she pressed her fingertips to her lips, as though ensuring that no words of protest would escape. She stared at Dominic with wide eyes, her mind racing.

Dominic was wrong! She knew he was Jason's father, without a flicker of doubt. Janice had had no reason not to tell the truth when she'd reluctantly agreed to Winthrop Ames's pleas to name the father of her baby as a safeguard in the event of a medical emergency.

Even more, Janice had told her that the man had been celebrating the opening of his *own* law practice.

Dominic Bonelli was Jason's father.

Why, dear heaven, why was he shifting the responsibility to one of his brothers? The direction he was taking suited her just fine, though. There would be no fight for custody, no more danger of her losing her precious son.

But why was he doing this? It just didn't make sense.

Think, Tessa, she told herself. What else had Janice said about Dominic? It was so long ago, and her emotions had been in such turmoil that day.

Think.

Yes, wait, it was coming back to her now. Janice had said that Dominic considered money the most important thing in his life. He was handsome, a great lover, but he was hard, cold.

Janice had said that Dominic Bonelli had no soul.

"Ms. Russell?" Dominic said, snapping her back to attention. "Are you listening to me?"

"What? Oh, yes, of course I am. I can truthfully say, Mr. Bonelli, that I was *not* cognizant of the fact that one of your brothers fathered Jason."

"Yes, all right," he said, a weary quality to his voice, "I'll go with that, with reservations." He shook his head. "Damn, what a mess. Look, could we sit back down and discuss this?"

Good idea, Tessa thought, moving to the sofa. Her legs were trembling so badly, she felt as if she were about to topple over onto her nose.

Dominic sat down in the chair, then leaned forward, resting his elbows on his knees and making a steeple of his long fingers.

Las Vegas, his mind hammered. It had been a wild bash. He'd never engaged in such a reckless event before, nor since, that weekend. The details were fuzzy, which was understandable due to its having taken place over five years ago.

He'd been drinking, but not to excess, he was certain. *That* he would never do, no matter what the circumstances. He'd never turn the control of himself over to liquor. His brothers, however, had really been putting away the booze.

His brothers. One of them had obviously picked up Janice Russell and taken her to bed. None of the four cheated on their wives, but when drunk as a skunk, sound reason and decent values must have been drowned in the alcohol.

Which one was it? Frank, Vince, Benny or Joe? He'd like to wring his neck, whoever it was, that was for damn sure.

Well, the situation was now good old Dominic's to deal with. He was the head of the family, and had been since he was fourteen years old. He made the decisions, provided the guidance, had supported his mother, two sisters and four brothers, until each was able to stand on their own. He continued to provide for Delores, his mother, whom he respected more than he could say.

Come on, Bonelli, he admonished himself. *Your mind is wandering.* He was chasing around well-known facts to postpone having to address the next imperative issue at hand—the guarantee of Tessa Russell's silence.

"Well," he said, straightening and leaning back in the chair, "it would appear, Ms. Russell, that the ball is now in your court. How much money do you want in exchange for not divulging the fact that Jason's father is a Bonelli?"

Fury rose in Tessa like a building storm, gaining momentum with every beat of her heart.

"Get out of my house," she said, her voice shaking from anger. "Get out, don't ever come back and never contact me again. Go. Now."

Dominic sighed. "Let's cut to the chase, shall we? I'm really not in the mood to play games. I'll prepare a document for you to sign that will state that you will never divulge the identity of Jason's father. I realize it could be any one of four men, so it will be worded to say you won't reveal that a Bonelli is the father.

"The fake document in the file makes perfect sense, because while my brothers earn good money, I have far more than they do. Whether it was you, or someone you have no knowledge of who prepared the form, is now immaterial. I haven't been contacted, so it's between the two of us."

"You don't feel that a man has the right to know he has a son?" Tessa felt she had to ask, though she knew such a question was strange coming from someone with so much to lose.

"Under the circumstances? No."

"Who appointed you master over people's lives?" Tessa said, her voice rising.

"Fate. I've been the head of my family since our father died when I was fourteen. My authority isn't questioned. *I* have decided how this will be handled, and that's the way it will be. I repeat, Ms. Russell, how much money do you want?"

Tessa got to her feet. "Leave my home!"

"I almost believe you don't want to be paid off," he said, retrieving his briefcase and getting to his feet. "Almost." He glanced around the room. "I'm quite sure you'll come up with a sizable figure in a few days. That's fine. The boy is a part of my family, therefore I feel a sense of responsibility toward him. Bonellis don't live like this, not anymore. Some money could do wonders for this place."

"You are the most despicable man I've ever had the misfortune to meet," she said, wrapping her hands around her elbows.

"Despicable? Yes, I've been told that a time or two." He crossed the room to the door, then turned to look at her. "You *are* going to follow me downstairs, aren't you? Lock the door behind me? After all, you have a Bonelli in your safekeeping, a fact I won't idly stand by and allow you to take lightly."

Trembling with anger, Tessa followed Dominic from the room and down the stairs. A thousand scathing words tumbled through her mind, but she was unable to speak due to her rage.

At the door, Dominic looked at her once again. "While I'm preparing the document you're to sign, I'll be waiting to hear from you regarding your price." He left the house.

Tessa fumbled with the lock with shaking hands, then finally clicked it into place. She made her way to the stairs, then sank onto the bottom step, resting her forehead on her knees.

Janice's voice echoed in her mind.

The man has no soul.

The man has no soul.

"Dear God," she whispered to the night, "Janice was right."

During the next two weeks, Dominic was aware that his level of tension was building steadily. His temper was on a short fuse, and Gladys had threatened to quit on four occasions.

His stress was due, he knew, to the lack of communication from Tessa Russell. He'd stayed late at the office one night to personally prepare the document for her to sign, not wishing anyone else to know of its existence. There was, however, a blank space on the form for the amount of money to be paid to Tessa in exchange for her silence.

In the middle of the morning that marked two weeks and three days since he'd last seen Tessa, Dominic tossed his pen onto the open file on his desk. He muttered an earthy expletive and got to his feet.

Walking to the sparkling-clean floor-to-ceiling windows, he shoved his hands into his pockets and stared unseeing at the view before him.

Why, he wondered for the umpteenth time, hadn't Tessa made her move? Until money changed hands and the document was signed, she was a threat. She had control of the situation by keeping him on tenterhooks.

He narrowed his eyes in anger.

Dominic Bonelli, he inwardly fumed, was not controlled by anyone, or anything. *Enough was enough.* Tessa Russell was obviously playing some sort of game, and he'd reached the end of his patience. He was taking the ball back into *his* court.

He strode to his chair, sat down and began to drum a rhythm on the top of the desk.

As a plan began to take shape in his mind, he nodded in satisfaction. It was risky, but a helluva lot better than enduring Tessa's silence. The type of compensation he was now contemplating could be money down the drain if she ultimately refused to sign the document. But by going with the new program, he'd have leverage, something tangible to help apply pressure for her signature.

Besides, he mused, he'd meant what he'd said. Tessa's house was clean, but shabby. Bonellis did not now, nor would they ever again, live with threadbare furniture and peeling paint.

Two objectives could be accomplished, hopefully, with his new idea.

With his jaw set in a determined line, he reached for the receiver.

Tessa turned the book around to show the brightly colored picture to the dozen children before her. They were sitting on the floor, each on a throw rug, watching her with rapt attention where she was perched on a low stool.

"Wow," a little girl said. "I'd like to live in a big castle like that."

"You have to be a princess, or queen, or something, Sarah," a boy said. "That's the rules of castles."

"I can live there if I wanna," Sarah said. "You don't know everything, Jeremiah."

"I know castle stuff," he said.

Tessa smiled, deciding to allow the debate to continue for a bit. Story hour was scheduled for after lunch each day. It provided time for the children's meals to settle, plus, more often than not, some of the kids curled up on their fluffy rugs and fell asleep.

To declare that it was nap time, Tessa had discovered early on, created an instant fuss and a chorus of objections. The way she did it now, those in need of sleep would drift off, and the others listened to the story.

Patty and Emma were tending to cleaning the kitchen from lunch, while Tessa had taken charge of story hour, her favorite time of the day.

"Maybe," another little girl said, "if you move into a castle, that makes you a princess right now, 'cause you live there."

"That's dumb," Jeremiah said.

"Is not," Sarah said.

Tessa's mind wandered as more voices joined the castle controversy.

Two weeks and three days, counting this one, she thought. That's how long it had been since Dominic Bonelli had paid his late-night visit. Surely he was intelligent enough to have deduced by now that she had no intention of asking him for money. She wanted nothing from him, *nothing,* except to be left alone.

She'd sign his damnable document guaranteeing her silence if he insisted upon it, but he'd have to come to her and ask for the coveted signature. He was no longer a threat to her and Jason.

What she didn't know, would probably never understand, was why Dominic had so quickly placed the responsibility of Jason's paternity onto one of his brothers. He'd strongly stated that *he* would never act in such an irresponsible manner, yet she knew he had. Perhaps Dominic was not capable of admitting a human weakness of any kind.

He was so cold, hard, aloof. It was, she supposed, totally unacceptable to him to acknowledge an error in judgment. But, dear heaven, when that slip in control had resulted in a beautiful child like Jason, how could Dominic deny the truth as he was doing? *Jason was his son.*

Because the man has no soul, she thought. It was incredibly sad. How empty Dominic Bonelli's life must be. He'd spoken of having been responsible for his large family from an early age. *Responsible.* That was admirable; he'd taken on a tremendous burden at fourteen years old. But did he *feel* anything toward that family except a sense of responsibility? Did he love them?

For Pete's sake, Tessa, she admonished herself, who cared? She was wasting mental energy wondering about the depth of Dominic Bonelli's emotions. Ridiculous. His outer shell was handsome, compelling, but within he was empty. That was *his* problem.

"Tessa, Tessa," Jeremiah yelled. "Aren't you gonna read the story?"

"What?" she said. "Oh, of course."

She turned the book back around, placed it on her knees and began to read.

An hour later, Patty and Emma took the children to the play area outside, while Tessa prepared the afternoon snack. As she was slicing an apple, the doorbell rang. She hurried from the kitchen to answer the summons.

On the other side of the locked screen door was a man appearing to be in his mid-twenties and who had blond hair, blue eyes and freckles. He was wearing jeans, a T-shirt and a smile.

"Hello," Tessa said, matching his smile. "How may I help you?"

As the man opened his mouth to reply, Tessa glanced over his shoulder and read the name of the company painted on the door of the truck parked beyond the front walkway.

"I'm Jeff, from—"

"Bonelli Painting and Restoration," Tessa said, in unison with him.

"Yes, ma'am," Jeff said.

"Bonelli Painting and Restoration?" Tessa repeated, her voice rising. "What in heaven's name are you doing here?"

Jeff's smile slid off his chin and he frowned. "I came to inspect your house, top to bottom, inside and out. You know, gather data on what needs to be done to make this place shipshape." He smiled again. "Okay?"

Tessa planted her hands on her hips and narrowed her eyes. "No, it is *not* okay. I didn't ask for an inspection of that sort, nor do I want one. You can march right back to town, and inform Mr. Bonelli of that fact."

"Oh," Jeff said, rubbing one hand over his chin. "Which one?"

"Tucson, of course."

"No, no, not which town, which Mr. Bonelli? I mean, it was Frank who told me to come out here, but maybe Vince told *him*. I don't know where the original order came from. It could have been Benny or Joe Bonelli. All four own Bonelli Painting and Restoration. So, who do you want me to go back and holler at?"

"Pick one," Tessa yelled. "Just make it clear that I don't want anybody from that company on my property."

"Yes, ma'am," Jeff said, raising both hands and backing up. "You betcha. No problem. I'm outta here." He turned and sprinted to the truck.

Tessa didn't move until the vehicle disappeared in a cloud of dust, then she stomped back into the kitchen. She picked up an apple and began to slice it with more force than was necessary.

Dominic Bonelli was behind this insulting maneuver, she fumed. He'd made several derogatory remarks about the condition of her house, tossing in the tidbit that Bonellis didn't live like this anymore.

Since she hadn't contacted him regarding the amount of money he expected her to demand in exchange for her silence, Dominic had apparently decided to take it upon himself to make improvements to the home where the *secret* Bonelli offspring lived.

"Oh-h-h, the nerve of that man," she said under her breath.

Well, she'd set him straight quickly enough. Once Jeff returned with her message, the whole group of Bonellis would know that Tessa Russell didn't want any part of them.

What had Dominic told his brothers? she wondered, as she made banana-fingers. What explanation had he given for requesting an inspection of Rainbow's End? Knowing him, he'd probably just barked the order, and his four brothers had clicked their heels and saluted, no questions asked.

Oh, who cared? She wasn't wasting one more minute thinking about the arrogant, pushy, drop-dead gorgeous Dominic.

With a decisive nod, she reached for a cluster of green grapes.

"That's the scoop, Dom," Frank Bonelli said. The receiver to the telephone was propped between his head and shoulder. "Tessa Russell ran Jeff off."

Dominic's hold on the receiver tightened. "Damn it, that woman is driving me crazy."

"What's going on?" Frank said. "I didn't think anything of it when you told me to get a thorough inspection done at this Rainbow's End place. You send work our way all the time. But that woman obviously doesn't want any part of it, or us. Did you get your signals crossed?"

"Look, I'll take care of Tessa Russell. Have Jeff go back out there tomorrow morning. I'll meet him at Rainbow's End at nine o'clock."

"Whatever," Frank said. "This sure doesn't make sense, Dom."

"Don't worry about it," Dominic said. "Goodbye, Frank."

Dominic slammed down the receiver and got to his feet. In the next instant, he sank back onto his chair, deciding that Tessa Russell wasn't going to cause him to pace the floor of his office again.

Frank had asked him if he'd gotten his signals crossed. Hell, he didn't know. He couldn't even begin to figure out the woman. And he had absolutely no idea why she hadn't contacted him to name her price.

He'd gotten so frustrated while waiting to hear from her, he'd decided to regain control of the situation by spending the damn money *for* her, in the manner *he* felt most appropriate.

Jason was a Bonelli, and the house where he was being raised needed a vast number of improvements. Tessa's silence would be bought, and Jason would be living in a proper environment.

It was a clever plan, an excellent plan. He'd be secure in the knowledge that the hush money wasn't being spent on frivolous things, and that the ultimate recipient would be the son of one of his brothers. Yes, it was very clever, indeed.

Until, Dominic thought, his temper flaring again, Tessa Russell had pitched her fit when Jeff had arrived at her house. Lord, she was difficult to deal with. He just couldn't get a handle on what made her tick, and he didn't like that, not one damn bit.

Well, as of nine o'clock tomorrow morning, Ms. Russell was going to start doing things *his* way.

"Get off of my porch," Tessa said through the screen door. "Get off of my entire property. If you don't leave within the next three seconds, I'm going to call the police."

"I'm gone," Jeff said.

"Don't move, Jeff," Dominic said, his jaw clenched. "There's been a small misunderstanding, that's all. Ms. Russell and I will have this straightened out in a few minutes."

"We certainly will not," she said, "because I refuse to discuss it with you. Three seconds, Mr. Bonelli."

"Tessa," Dominic said, "I can't believe that you'd want the children in your care telling their parents that an argument took place here, would you? The mothers and fathers might question whether this is a calm, peaceful environment for their children."

"You're despicable," she said.

"*You* are stubborn. Open the door and let me in so we can talk privately, with no little ears to hear and little mouths to carry tales."

Tessa glowered at Dominic for a long moment, then unlocked the door. As Dominic entered, leaving Jeff on the porch, Tessa spun around and marched across the living room, through the kitchen, and into the small office beyond.

She sat down behind the narrow desk, clutched her hands on the top and nodded toward a chair.

"Sit," she said. "Speak. Fast."

Dominic settled onto the chair. "Do you want me to roll over? Play dead?"

"Be my guest," she said ever so sweetly.

"You're being very difficult, Tessa."

"Ms. Russell to you . . . *Dominic*. Let me make this clear for the last time. I do not want any of your money. I do not want *anything* from you. I'll sign your document saying I won't divulge the identity of Jason's father. All right? In return, you are to assure me that you and the entire Bonelli clan never contact me again. In short, you can take your money, your paint, your restoration—and stuff it!"

Dominic planted his elbows on the worn arms of the chair and made a steeple of his fingers. He stared at Tessa over the top of his fingers.

She meant it, he thought incredulously. She honestly didn't want money from him. He had never met anyone like Tessa Russell before. She was incredibly naive, and obviously didn't realize that money was the key to unlocking the doors a person wished to pass through. It was the ace in the hole that could win the hand holding power and control.

He shook his head.

"Well," he said, "you may, or may not, learn the true facts of life in the years to come, but that's not my problem. I accept your decision to sign the affidavit with no monetary compensation. I'll draft a new document."

"Agreed. Goodbye."

"Not so fast," he said, raising one hand. "There is Jason to consider here. Your son, Tessa."

"It's Ms. Russell. I'm very aware that Jason is my son."

"He's also a Bonelli."

"Which is of no importance."

"Ah, but it is. I feel responsible for Jason because his father is one of my brothers. That responsibility includes seeing that Jason is living in a proper home, and receiving proper care."

"Are you insinuating that—"

"Hold it. Don't go off on one of your rips. I'm not questioning your care of the boy, Tessa," he said quietly. "It's obvious to me, and would be to anyone who might observe you, that you're a wonderful mother who is devoted to her son. I admire and respect that."

"Oh," she said, feeling a warm flush on her cheeks. How absurd. She was registering a sense of pride and pleasure at hearing that Dominic approved of how she was raising Jason. "Well, thank you."

"However," he went on, "this house is falling down around your ears."

"It is not. It's a tad old, that's all."

"Did the roof leak during the monsoons?"

"Not much, just here and there," she said, folding her arms across her breasts. "It's really none of your business."

"It is when a Bonelli is under that roof. Are you going to deny your son a better home because of your stubbornness? And this place needs painting. Aren't you being a little selfish?"

"Do you think money and your clinical sense of responsibility is the answer to everything?"

"It certainly is in this case. Jason is being offered comforts that you're not allowing him to have. I've provided these types of things for all the Bonellis over the years. Jason has a right to have them, too."

"And how would you suggest I explain the sudden financial windfall that enabled me to fix up my house?"

"We'll think of something. You won a contest and the prize was a new roof and some painting. That's a small glitch, and easily solved. The major issue here is my responsibility for a Bonelli, and your being willing to allow your son a more comfortable home."

"Damn you," Tessa said.

Dominic got to his feet. "I'll take that as your having seen the light. Jeff will begin the inspection immediately. Goodbye, Tessa." He left the room.

"It's Ms. Russell," she said wearily.

Chapter Six

During the remainder of that day and the major portion of the next, Friday, Jeff conducted his inspection of Rainbow's End.

Tessa gritted her teeth and ignored him, even though he seemed to pop up wherever she was at the moment. He carried a clipboard with some sort of form attached, where he continually made notations.

Jeff whistled while he worked, which grated on Tessa's nerves. Even more unsettling were the mumbled comments she'd hear him make, such as "geez," "whew," "grim," "not good, not good," and "holy smokes."

On Saturday morning, Tessa announced to Jason that they were going to town. Her need to get away from the house was overwhelming.

They had a marvelous day, going to the zoo, having lunch at a fast-food restaurant and shopping for new tennis shoes for Jason.

Sunday, she dipped into the budgeted emergency fund and took Jason to Old Tucson, a replica of a turn-of-the-century western town where a movie was presently being filmed.

In addition to enjoying the added attraction of the Hollywood film crew, they watched the regularly scheduled performance of the shoot-out between the good guys and bad guys, with stuntmen making dramatic plunges off rooftops and from the backs of galloping horses.

By Sunday evening, after an exhausted and happy Jason was tucked into bed for the night, Tessa felt more like herself, her frazzled nerves calmed. She was pleasantly tired, knew she'd sleep well and had precious memories of the events shared with Jason.

Settled on the sofa with a thick book, she jerked in surprise when the telephone rang. She narrowed her eyes as she reached for the receiver, deciding it better not be Dominic disturbing her peace of mind again.

"Hello?" she said, into the receiver.

"Dominic Bonelli."

Tessa pursed her lips and counted slowly to ten.

"Tessa?"

"This is Ms. Russell. What do you want?"

Dominic chuckled, and a strange and unexpected tingle danced along Tessa's spine as she heard the rich, masculine sound.

"A bit testy tonight, are we?" Dominic said, amusement evident in his voice. "Perhaps I should apologize for disturbing you."

"Perhaps you should," she said coolly.

"All right, Ms. Russell, I apologize for interrupting your quiet evening at home."

"Oh." She was, she realized, rather flustered that Dominic had actually apologized. "Well, I... Was there something important you wished to discuss with me?"

"Several things, as a matter of fact. First up, I'd like to suggest we call a truce on this name business. You're Tessa and I'm Dominic. After all, there's no need for the formality of the Ms. and Mr. Agreed?"

Tessa smiled in spite of herself. There was something different about Dominic tonight. The brisk and arrogant edge to his voice was gone, replaced by a more relaxed tone. She had the distinct impression that he was still smiling after having executed that sexy chuckle.

"Yes, all right," she said. "I agree."

"Good." He paused. "Did you have a nice weekend? How's the boy? No, erase that. How's *Jason?*"

"Oh, he's fine. We had a marvelous weekend because I took him to... You don't really want to know all this."

"Actually," he said slowly, "I do. I'd like to hear about your outings."

Tessa moved the receiver from her ear and stared at it for a moment with the irrational thought that she might be able to peer into Dominic's brain.

He was acting so unlike himself—at least, unlike the Dominic she knew. There was even a warmth in his voice she'd never heard before.

Oh, Tessa, don't be silly, she admonished herself, placing the receiver back to her ear. She was thinking the way someone might who had known Dominic Bonelli for a long time, and who was suddenly aware of a change in his demeanor. In actuality, she didn't know him at all.

Then again, that wasn't entirely true. He had, in fact, had a shadowy place in her life for over five years, ever since she'd signed the guardianship document so she could bring Jason home from the hospital, and had seen the information in the file naming Dominic as Jason's father.

But *this* Dominic? The one speaking to her now? He really wanted to hear about a trip to the zoo? This was a facet of him she hadn't encountered before.

"Tessa?"

She mentally shrugged. "Well, okay, you asked for it. On Saturday..."

As Tessa related the events of the weekend, she realized she was enjoying chatting with Dominic. He was a wonderful listener. He made comments in appropriate places, asked questions and laughed several times at Jason's antics.

While Dominic's chuckle had caused a tingling sensation to course through her, the deep timbre of his laughter created a heat, a swirling, churning heat, low within her.

It was disconcerting and unsettling, to say the least. And enough was enough.

"And there you have it," she said. "A synopsis of a weekend in the fast lane."

"Delightful, but you must be exhausted."

"Totally. Jason was asleep the minute his head touched the pillow."

"Thank you for sharing all that with me, Tessa," Dominic said quietly. "I enjoyed it."

"You're welcome," she said, still a bit surprised.

A silence fell that was charged with a current of sexuality. Even though they were only talking on the telephone, it was there, a nearly palpable entity.

Dominic finally cleared his throat, breaking the eerie and sensuous spell.

"Well, I'll only keep you a moment longer," he said, "so you can get some rest. I wanted to let you know that a crew will be arriving at Rainbow's End first thing in the morning to begin work on repairing the roof.

"Since I'll be writing the checks to my brothers' company, I simply told them I'm the executor of an estate that had a will stipulating that the spending of funds bequeathed to you be controlled and approved by me."

Tessa frowned. *Back to reality, Ms. Russell,* she told herself. Dominic had just put on his attorney uniform again.

"I see," she said.

"I can't dictate who is to be part of the work crew without raising questions. Therefore, if any of my brothers show up there, be certain that Jason doesn't have any direct contact with them. I don't want them to notice the Bonelli ear, for lack of a better thing to call it."

"Nor do I," she said. Damn the man, he was still doing it. He was denying that he was Jason's father, pushing the role onto one of his brothers. *This* was the Dominic she knew—cold, commanding, unwilling to admit he had any human weaknesses. "I assure you that Jason won't be any more visible than the rest of the children."

"Fine."

"Have you prepared the document you wish me to sign?"

"Not entirely. Once all the improvements and repairs have been completed at Rainbow's End, I'll be able to make a detailed list of what you received in exchange for your silence."

"Regarding the fact that one of your brothers is Jason's father."

"As I told you, the wording will stipulate that you won't name *any* Bonelli as the boy's father, since we don't know which of my brothers was involved with your sister."

"I'll sign whatever you wish," Tessa said wearily. "Do remember to include the clause that no Bonelli is to contact me in the future about this, or any other matter."

"Of course. That's settled then. Good night, Tessa. Sleep well."

"Good night."

She replaced the receiver and picked up the novel. Several minutes later, she realized she'd read the same paragraph three times and had no idea what it had said.

Smacking the book onto the sofa cushion, she glowered at the telephone, and decided to go to bed.

Dominic lost track of time as he stared at the receiver long after he'd put it back in place. As seconds ticked into countless minutes, the frown knitting his dark eyebrows deepened.

What in the hell had come over him? he fumed. He'd called Tessa Russell with the intention of telling her to keep Jason away from any of his brothers who might be part of the crew working on her roof. That

was to be the full extent of the purpose of the call—
short and sweet.

So where had all the chitchat come from? And if
that wasn't ridiculous enough, he'd urged her to tell
him about her weekend spent with a five-year-old kid!

He lunged to his feet and began to pace the large
expanse of his expensively furnished living room.

The worst part was that he'd *enjoyed* every bit of
the inane conversation.

Dominic stopped his trek and ran one hand over the
back of his neck. The remembrance of Tessa's femi-
ninely lilting voice and the wind-chime delicacy of her
laughter echoed in his head, causing an uncomfortable tightening low in his body.

He slouched back into the high-backed leather
chair, and shook his head.

Bonelli, he admonished himself, *you're losing it.*
Tessa was a problem he was in the process of solving.
That she happened to be an attractive, refreshingly
honest woman, was incidental.

His behavior on the telephone was ludicrous. Tessa
wasn't even his type, damn it. He dated sophisticated
career women who were single, independent and had
every intention of remaining so. They weren't interested in marriage, babies or hearth and home. He slept
with some, no strings attached, and a good time was
had by all.

But Tessa? Sophisticated? Not even close. Maybe
she dated, but as far as he knew, she operated in a
narrow existence centered on Jason and Rainbow's
End. Oh, she had a temper, and could spit fire when
pushed too far, but there was an innocence about her
that caused a man to want to protect her from...well,
from men like himself.

"Oh, hell," he said.

Did he need a vacation? he wondered. He'd been working long hours, and had spent the weekend buried in legal files.

Yes, that was it. He'd have gladly listened to a lengthy dissertation about the weather, if only to mentally escape from legalese for a while. Hence, he'd allowed himself to get caught up in a tale of trips to the zoo and Old Tucson. Fine. That was now perfectly understandable.

With a satisfied nod, Dominic reached for the file on the end table. He flipped it open, then stared into space.

It had sounded as though Tessa and Jason had really enjoyed their outings. After having been to Old Tucson, Jason would no doubt spend the next several days, or even weeks, pretending he was a rough-tough cowboy. Did he have a pint-size Stetson? Some cowboy boots? Had he ever had a ride on a real horse?

"What difference does it make?" Dominic said aloud. "Who cares?"

He didn't know if his own nieces and nephews had ever been on a horse. He'd never asked, because being the entertainment chairman for the Bonelli clan wasn't part of his job description.

His responsibility was to be certain that everyone in the family had what they needed to succeed; all the material necessities while pursuing their individual goals.

And now? There was another Bonelli suddenly on the scene—Jason Robert Russell. He was faced with the responsibility of bringing Jason's standard of living up to the proper level. As usual, he was proceeding with the program, the situation was under his command.

Would a horse frighten a little kid like Jason? Perhaps it would be better to have him ride a pony instead. Did Tessa realize that? Surely she wouldn't put Jason on a huge horse and scare the living daylights out of him, would she? Maybe he should speak to her about that....

"A Fix-Up-Your-House contest?" Patty said to Tessa. "And you won?"

"Sure did," Tessa said, not looking directly at Patty or Emma. "Isn't that something?" Her nose was going to grow. It was probably written all over her face that she was making up the whole thing. "Lucky me, huh?"

"That's wonderful," Emma said. "I won a frozen pizza once, but this is the big time."

Patty laughed. "Not only do you get a new roof, Tessa, but we get to ogle some very nice masculine bodies. Did you see the physiques on those guys outside? There are...what? Four of them? Five? And every one is built like a dream."

"Shame on you, Patty," Tessa said, smiling.

"I may be fifty-four, but I'm not dead," she said. "There's no harm in looking. You, Tessa Russell, would do well to be friendly to those hunks. You need a social life, some dates. Jason is a sweetheart, but there should be more in a woman's existence than working and taking care of her son."

"I'm perfectly happy the way I am," Tessa said, raising both hands.

"You just *think* you are," Patty said, folding her arms over her ample bosom. "Right, Emma? Our girl needs a man."

"Absolutely," Emma said, nodding. "And there's a splendid selection working on your roof even as we speak."

"Oh, good grief," Tessa said, rolling her eyes heavenward. "I'm going to go prepare the morning snack. There are a dozen little demons awaiting your attention in the play yard, ladies. Goodbye." She spun around and headed for the kitchen.

Tessa performed her task by rote as her mind drifted back in time, colliding with painful memories.

She'd *had* a man in her life once, and had ended up with a broken heart and shattered dreams.

Cliff had eaten regularly at the restaurant where she worked as a waitress. He was good-looking, friendly and very charming. Although initially she had refused his invitations to various outings, she finally relented, and they began to date steadily.

She hadn't realized how alone and lonely she'd been until Cliff had become part of her life, a *very* important part. She'd fallen in love with him, eagerly surrendered her virginity at twenty years old, and daydreamed about being married to Cliff, having his baby, being part of a real family again.

Then after six months, Cliff had casually informed her that his *wife* was becoming suspicious of the many hours he was away from home, and he couldn't see Tessa again. *Thanks for the fun, sugar. See ya.*

"Wife," Tessa muttered, as she sliced an orange. "The creep had a wife."

When the pain of Cliff's betrayal had dimmed enough to enable her not to cry herself to sleep each night, anger had set in.

It was rip-roaring, mad-as-hell anger.

At herself.

When her parents had been killed, her life had been placed in the control of other people. She had had no say, no choices. She could only do as she was told, like an obedient robot.

Savoring her freedom when she'd gone out on her own at eighteen, she'd been determined to take charge of her existence. She'd been doing just fine, until Cliff. Then, foolish and gullible idiot that she'd been, she'd placed her happiness in his hands for safekeeping, and he'd crushed it without a second thought.

Never again, she'd vowed. Never again would she relinquish control of her life, allow anyone to dictate whether she laughed with joy, or sobbed in sorrow.

"No, Patty, Emma," Tessa said aloud, to the empty room. "I most definitely do *not* need a man in my life."

A sudden, unexpected, and unwelcomed image of Dominic flickered in Tessa's mental vision.

She narrowed her eyes.

And at the top of the Most *Un*wanted List, would be Dominic Bonelli!

Chapter Seven

A few minutes later, Tessa jerked in surprise as a ladder suddenly appeared outside the kitchen window, then thudded against the house. She rinsed her hands, dried them quickly and headed out the back door.

A man was by the ladder, operating the mechanism that would extend it to its full height, allowing him access to the roof of the two-story house.

And the man was a Bonelli.

Tessa stopped and scrutinized him. He was dressed in jeans, a T-shirt and was wearing a baseball cap. He wasn't quite as tall as Dominic, nor were his shoulders as wide, but his rough-hewn features, even in profile, shouted the fact that this was one of Dominic's brothers. He had the same straight nose, square jaw, tawny skin and the hair she could see at the edges of the cap was thick and black.

Which one of the four was he? she wondered. And how would he feel if he knew that his authoritative older brother was placing the responsibility of fathering Jason on him, or one of the other three brothers?

Dominic's refusal to acknowledge his own son was so wrong, so unbelievably wrong. Granted, it meant that the threat to her and Jason was removed from their existence, but how could a man do such a cold-hearted thing?

Shaking her head, Tessa walked to where the man was still fiddling with the ladder.

"I'd like to talk to you," she said, deciding to omit a pleasant greeting. She didn't want these people here, and she had no intention of pretending that she did.

The man turned to look at her, a wide smile on his face.

There were the dark eyes and long lashes, Tessa noticed. He was good-looking but not quite as ruggedly handsome as Dominic. And there, clear as day, was the small dip on the top of his right ear.

"Good morning, ma'am," he said. "I'm Frank Bonelli. You must be Tessa Russell."

"Yes, I am," she said, folding her arms over her breasts. There was no hint of a smile on her face. "I have some concerns regarding this project, Mr. Bonelli."

Frank took off his cap, shoved his hand through his hair and settled the cap back into place. His smile never wavered.

"Well, now, we can't have you worrying about anything, ma'am. Oh, and call me Frank. We Bonellis are a friendly bunch."

Oh, ha! Tessa thought. Dominic Bonelli was *not* friendly. He was arrogant, pushy and rude. Of course, he *had* been extremely nice during the majority of that strange telephone conversation last night.

"Yes, well, Frank," she said coolly, "it occurs to me that in order to put a new roof on a house, the old roof has to come off. Therefore, the worn shingles have to get from there—" she pointed heavenward "—to here." She pointed to the ground. "I have a dozen children playing in the side yard. I can't have shingles flying all over the place. So, let's just cancel this job, shall we?"

Frank frowned. "I've never had anyone try to talk me out of fixing their roof before. Most people are glad to know that they won't be running a bucket brigade inside the house the next time it rains."

"I'm not most people. I think it would be best if you and your crew just packed up and left. The safety of these children is far more important than any inconvenience I might experience during a rainstorm."

"Now, Tessa... May I call you Tessa? That is sure a pretty name. Tessa, you come along with me, and I'll show you why you don't have a thing to worry about." He moved past her. "Come on."

"But," she started, then hurried after him.

At the opposite side of the house from the play yard, four men were busily hammering together large sheets of plywood.

"Yo!" Frank yelled.

The four men stopped and looked at him questioningly.

Two more Bonellis, Tessa realized. Goodness, a person certainly could pick them out of a crowd. They wore their hair shorter than Dominic, just as Frank did, and the dips in their ears were clearly visible.

Even without the telltale ear, the family resemblance was remarkable. Yet, again, these two weren't quite as tall, or well built, or as handsome as Dominic. She couldn't quite put her finger on exactly what Dominic had that the others didn't, but it was *something*.

"Guys," Frank said, "this is Tessa, the lady of the house. Tessa, you know Jeff. Those two uglies are my brothers, Benny and Vince, and that weird-looking fella is Clyde. No kiddin', his mother actually named him Clyde."

"Hello," Tessa said, nodding slightly.

She was answered with hellos, pleased to meet yous, pleasure, ma'am and broad smiles.

Tessa smiled in spite of herself, deciding it was impossible to stay totally grumpy when surrounded by such cheerful, friendly people.

"Now then, Jeff," Frank said, "you explain to Tessa what you guys are doing there. She's worried about shingles flying around and maybe hurting some of the kids." He looked at Tessa. "We sent Jeff to school for talking lessons, so he could explain stuff to folks." He chuckled and winked at her.

Jeff cleared his throat and smoothed his T-shirt over his chest as though he were about to deliver the inaugural address.

Tessa laughed softly, mentally admitting defeat of her attempt to be stern.

"We are presently building," Jeff commenced, "a large pen where the old shingles will be placed. We'll construct a slide, of sorts, out of heavy tarps from the roof to here so we can zoom the old stuff down right where we want them. You don't have to fret one iota about your kiddies."

"Oh," Tessa said.

"Go back to sleep, Jeff," Frank said, then turned to Tessa. "You have two layers of shingles on your roof. City code says you can have up to three layers. Thing is, at the first sign of trouble down the road, everything has to come off and started fresh. Dom said to do a tear-off... that's going down to the sheathing under all the shingles... now. He wants a whole new roof, first layer."

"Oh," Tessa said again. "What if it rains while it's torn down to that sheathing?"

"No problem," Frank said. "We do it in sections. Tear off, replace, tear off, replace. We never leave at the end of the day with the roof in a condition that would be a disaster if it rained. Okay?"

"Yes, thank you. I appreciate your time, patience and information. Goodbye." She spun around and hurried away.

Back in the kitchen, she rolled her eyes heavenward.

Great, she inwardly fumed, she'd just made a complete fool of herself. She'd marched outside like Miss High-and-Mighty, her nose in the air, and told Frank Bonelli to take his shingles and go away. She'd come across as a total idiot.

Well, now wait a minute. Maybe she hadn't appeared as dumb as all that. Frank, and his whole crew, as a matter of fact, had been friendly, warm and outgoing. They'd reacted as though her concern for the safety of the children in regard to zooming shingles was perfectly reasonable. They'd addressed the question with a delightful dose of humor, and everything was fine.

The Bonelli brothers, as well as Jeff and Clyde, obviously had a special bond. There was an easiness amongst them, as well as respect for one another, a family feeling.

And Dominic? she wondered. When he was with his brothers, was he as relaxed and ready to smile as they were? Did he let down his authoritative guard, change out of his attorney uniform and become one of the boys? Surely he realized how fortunate he was to be surrounded by a large and loving family. Didn't he?

Tessa shook her head and resumed the task of preparing the children's snack.

What difference did it make to her whether or not Dominic had enough sense and sensitivity to appreciate his family? None, absolutely none. She didn't even like the man, for Pete's sake.

So why was she wasting her time thinking about him? Good question, and she had no idea what the answer was.

With a cluck of self-disgust, she headed for the play yard to round up the children for their morning snack.

Just before seven o'clock that evening, Tessa sat on the bench swing on the front porch, pushing it gently back and forth. She smiled as she watched Jason playing in the yard. He was using a straw broom as a horse and was galloping around. He'd been in a cowboy mode ever since the trip to Old Tucson.

Tessa sighed in contentment. It was a beautiful evening. There was a cool breeze whispering along the porch, and a gorgeous sunset was beginning to streak across the heavens with vibrant colors, each shade melting into the next like softening butter.

Jason was yipping, yelling and occasionally whinnying, leading her to believe he was alternating between being a horse and a cowboy.

What an enchanting world of innocence and imagination little boys existed in, she mused. These were such precious years, so special. All too soon, Jason would grow up and be forced to face the complexities, stresses and pressures of adulthood.

Her youth had ended abruptly when she was fourteen, due to her parents being killed, and soon after, Janice had been lost to her, too.

Dominic had had his boyhood cut short, as well, at the same age she had been when she had found herself confronting cold reality. While she had felt abandoned and so terribly alone, he had been placed in a position of responsibility far greater than any fourteen-year-old boy should have to assume.

He apparently had achieved his goals of providing for his family. He, himself, was a prominent attorney, and his brothers had their own business, which was no small accomplishment. Were there sisters, too? A mother?

And now there was Jason, another Bonelli, whom Dominic felt responsible for. Would he ever acknowledge that Jason was his son?

A part of her hoped and prayed that he wouldn't, as the threat of his seeking custody of Jason would once again haunt her.

But another section of her mind was registering sorrow that Jason would never be allowed to interact with his father, have a male influence in his life. And there, too, was a flicker of sadness that Dominic wouldn't experience the exquisite joy of having his son wrap his little arms around Dominic's neck and say, "I love you, Daddy."

Her mind, Tessa decided, was playing push-me-pull-me. For her and Jason's future security, she *never* wanted Dominic to admit that Jason was his. Yet, for Dominic's sake, she—

Tessa's jumbled thoughts were cut off by the sound of an approaching vehicle and the billowing dust it was stirring up. A few minutes later, the car was close enough for her to recognize who was coming to Rainbow's End.

"Dominic," she whispered.

She started to rise, then settled back onto the swing, deciding she wasn't going to snap to attention just because the almighty Mr. Bonelli was gracing them with his arrogant presence. This was *her* home, he had not been invited, so let him come to her where she sat on the swing.

Tessa, you have an attitude, she admonished herself, laughing softly. The evening was too lovely to disrupt with hostility. She'd keep an open mind and discover the purpose of Dominic's visit. She was not, however, going to jump to her feet to greet him.

Dominic parked in front of the house, got out of the car, then reached back onto the seat for something Tessa couldn't see.

As he came around the front of the vehicle and into full view, carrying a shopping bag, her breath caught and a funny flutter danced along her spine.

Dominic was wearing faded jeans and a black knit shirt. The soft, nearly-white-in-places jeans hugged his narrow hips and accentuated the length and power of his legs. The shirt clung to his wide shoulders, broad chest, and the short sleeves circled muscled biceps.

While he had been drop-dead gorgeous in his attorney uniform, he was absolutely magnificent in casual clothes.

Tessa, she ordered herself, *get a grip.*

"Hello, Jason," Dominic said, strolling up the front walk. "Do you remember me?" He stopped and looked at the little boy.

"Whoa," Jason said, pulling back on the broom. He cocked his head to one side and studied Dominic. "You were here today doin' stuff to our roof."

Dominic laughed. The funny flutter Tessa had felt earlier reappeared within her, low and deep, at the sound of the rich, masculine laughter.

"No, those were my brothers," Dominic said. "We all look alike."

Not quite, Tessa thought. Dominic was a cut above the rest for some unexplainable reason.

"Oh," Jason said. "I wish I had a brother."

Tessa stiffened and frowned.

Jason wanted a brother? He'd never said anything like that to *her.* In fact, he'd never questioned the fact that he didn't have a father.

"Maybe someday you'll have a brother," Dominic said, "or a sister. I have two sisters."

"I don't think I'd like having a sister," Jason said. "They play with dolls and junk. I'm a cowboy."

"I thought you might be," Dominic said, nodding. "That's a great horse."

"Yep," Jason said, then turned and galloped across the yard.

As Dominic continued on his way to the porch, Tessa smiled at a spot above his right shoulder, deciding it was not a terrific idea to spend any more time staring at his physique displayed to perfection in those clothes.

"Good evening, Tessa," Dominic said, stepping onto the porch.

"Hello," she said pleasantly. "What brings you way out here? Would you care to sit down?" She gestured to one of the wicker chairs.

"Thank you," he said, then proceeded to settle next to her on the swing. He set the shopping bag on the porch at the end of the swing.

Tessa's eyes widened in surprise. She opened her mouth to object to his choice of seating, decided she'd sound like a prude, and snapped her mouth closed again.

So, fine, she thought, they'd share the swing. It was no big deal. It was just that she'd never realized before that it was so small. When Jason sat on the swing with her, his leg didn't press against hers as Dominic's was doing. But, no problem, she could handle this.

Maybe.

There was such incredible *heat* traveling from Dominic's leg into hers, then through her entire body. The heat swirled, then began to thrum in a steady pulse low within her.

Think about something else, she directed herself.

"My, my," she said, instantly realizing there was an odd, breathless quality to her voice. "Isn't this a lovely evening? The weather is so nice this time of year." She folded her hands in her lap.

Dominic spread one arm along the top of the swing, then set the swing in motion, moving it gently back and forth.

"Yes," he said, nodding. "Very nice."

A long, silent minute ticked by. Tessa slid a glance at Dominic, seeing his relaxed demeanor and the relaxed expression on his face as he looked at the sunset.

He was calm, cool and collected, she thought dismally, and she was rapidly becoming a nervous wreck. Not only did she have his leg to contend with, but now he'd added an arm that she was *extremely* aware of. What was Dominic up to? Why was he here?

"Why are you here?" she said, turning her head to look at him. That had sounded rude, but tough. She hadn't invited him, he hadn't called before coming, so she deserved to know what he wanted. "Dominic?"

"What?" He met her gaze. "I'm sorry. Between the rhythm of the swing and the spectacular sunset, I sort of mellowed out, I guess. I can't remember when I've taken the time to enjoy a sunset. Do you sit out here like this often?"

"Yes, every evening once it cools down from the summer heat. Despite his busy day, Jason still has a lot of energy left after dinner, and he likes to play in the yard." She laughed. "He talks me into playing catch with him, which is usually a disaster. I spend a great deal of time chasing after the balls I didn't manage to catch. I'm getting a reprieve tonight because he's a cowboy at the moment."

Dominic smiled. "When you told me you'd taken him to Old Tucson, I thought he'd probably be a cowboy for a while. Has he even been on a real horse?"

"He rode a pony around in a circle at one of those pony-ride things at the zoo. I don't think he's quite big enough for a full-size horse yet."

"Oh? Well, that's what I thought, too. You know, a pony ride would be fine, but a horse might frighten him."

Tessa frowned slightly. "You were thinking about Jason riding a pony?"

"It crossed my mind."

Why? Tessa wondered. Why would Dominic be using his mental energy on a topic so mundane as whether Jason should ride a horse or a pony?

"You still haven't said what brought you out here," she said.

"Well, there are a couple of reasons. First up, I wanted to make certain that everything went all right with the roof. I spoke with Frank, and he said you'd had some concerns, which he'd addressed, and everything had proceeded on schedule."

"Yes."

"I'm just double-checking," he said. Which was nuts. If Frank said things were fine, they were fine. Why was he here? Because he'd wanted to come, a fact he'd decided not to analyze.

"All is well," Tessa said, shrugging. "It's a tad noisy with the men hammering on the roof, but it's not that bad." She paused. "Your brothers are very nice. I met Frank, Benny and Vince. They're warm and friendly. Jeff and Clyde are pleasant, too."

Warm and friendly, Dominic mentally repeated. He had a sneaking suspicion that no one had ever used those words to describe *him.* Fine. He didn't have time for such things. But Vince, Benny and Frank were warm and friendly?

"I imagine you'll meet my brother Joe before the work is completed."

"Is he friendly, too?" Tessa asked, smiling.

"Damned if I know," he said gruffly. "I suppose he is. I've never thought about it."

"You don't know your own brothers' personality traits?"

"No. Yes. Like I said, I haven't given it much thought."

"Oh."

Another silent minute passed, then Dominic cleared his throat.

"Tessa, the other reason I came is that I want to officially apologize for having accused you of sending me the file about Jason. I was talking to an attorney friend of mine today, and he said that the closing of Winthrop Ames's law practice wasn't handled very well."

"Oh?"

"Apparently, his secretary had been with him for many years and was extremely upset by his death. Due to her emotional state, she didn't use proper judgment regarding some of the case files. An inventory list showed she'd mailed several files directly to people who should never have had them. I'm assuming Janice's file was one of those."

"I see," Tessa said slowly. "Well, that solves the mystery, at least. That poor woman must have been consumed by grief."

"Will you accept my apology?"

"Yes, of course. It wasn't necessary for you to drive all the way out here, Dominic." She smiled. "I accept apologies over the phone."

"Yes, well, there's a third item on my agenda. I figured Jason was a cowboy because of your outing and . . . what I mean is . . . Hell."

Tessa stared at him, her eyes widening slightly.

Dominic Bonelli, she thought incredulously, *was nervous.* This was yet another side to Dominic, one she'd never expected to see. There was a sudden vulnerability about him that was very human and *very* endearing.

"Dominic," she said, smiling softly, "what are you trying to say?"

He cleared his throat again. "I bought Jason a cowboy suit. It has a hat, shirt, pants, boots, but no guns. I didn't know how you felt about his having play-guns." He was talking too fast, damn it, blithering like an idiot. "I've never bought clothes for a kid before. For their birthdays and at Christmas, I give my nieces and nephews checks to go into their education funds. I hope the suit fits Jason. I thought I should ask you first, though, if it's all right for him to have it."

A sensation of warmth seemed to tiptoe around Tessa's heart, encircling it with a lovely caress.

"It's wonderful," she said, smiling. "He'll be so thrilled. Thank you, Dominic. Thank you very much. Why don't you call him up here and give him the surprise yourself?" She paused. "Well, I've now officially included you on the list of Bonellis who are warm and friendly."

Chapter Eight

With an earthy expletive, Dominic threw back the
blankets and left the bed. He strode naked across the
thick carpeting covering the floor of the large bedroom to one of the windows on the far wall.

Shoving aside a panel of the drapes, he stared out at
the peaceful night, oblivious to the breathtaking
spectacle of millions of stars glittering like diamonds
in the sky.

On Monday, he fumed, he'd visited Tessa at Rainbow's End. This was Wednesday. This was also the
third night in a row that he hadn't been able to sleep
for more than snatches at a time.

Because of Tessa Russell.

"Damn it," he said, dropping the drape back into
place.

He returned to the bed, stretched out, laced his hands beneath his head and glowered at a ceiling he couldn't see in the darkness.

Tessa Russell was driving him crazy. She'd taken up residence in his mind, refused to budge, and he'd had enough of this nonsense.

He'd *never* been preoccupied by lingering thoughts and images of a woman. *Never.*

So what in the hell was the matter with him?

All right, Bonelli, he thought, get your act together. He'd attack this situation as he would a complex legal matter. He'd mentally spread it out, examine the data, then analyze the conclusions he'd drawn.

Fine.

He'd gone to Rainbow's End on Monday evening on impulse, which was extremely out of character for him.

And as if that wasn't unsettling enough, he'd taken Jason a cowboy outfit that he'd shopped for himself. He'd actually done that; gone into the kids' section of a department store for the first time in his life, and spent an incredible amount of time selecting the clothes, as though they were the most important purchases he'd ever made.

"Hell," he said with a snort of self-disgust.

In the next instant, as if of its own volition, a smile tugged at his lips.

Man, oh, man, Jason had been so excited about that cowboy suit, it was a wonder he hadn't floated right off the porch. He'd been hopping around, shouting and clapping his hands. It had really been something to witness so much pure happiness bubbling out of such a little kid.

It had taken both Tessa and himself to peel off Jason's clothes and stuff him into the cowboy garb because the boy was wiggling around so much and urging them to hurry.

Then Tessa had insisted that Jason stand still long enough to properly thank Mr. Bonelli for his wonderful gift.

"Thank you, Mr. Bonelli," Jason had said, "a whole bunch. This is the bestis surprise I *ever* had."

"You're welcome, Jason. If it's all right with your mom, I'd like you to call me Dominic."

"Mom?"

"That's fine," Tessa said, nodding.

Jason cocked his head to one side and looked at Dominic.

"Are you my friend?" the little boy asked.

A strange tightness gripped Dominic's throat, and it was a long moment before he could answer.

"Yes, Jason," he had finally said, "I'm your friend." He'd extended his hand. "And *you* are *my* friend. Let's shake on it."

Dominic pulled his hands from beneath his head and curled the fingers of his right hand into a loose fist.

He could still remember the feel of Jason's small hand in his. It was so tiny, warm, soft, delivering a message of trust. He'd never shaken hands with a child before, and he'd been moved by the gesture. He had been reluctant to release Jason's hand.

"Can I go ride my horse now?" Jason had said, jumping up and down.

"Do it," Dominic said, laughing.

Jason dashed off, and Tessa's laughter mingled with Dominic's, seeming to fill the porch, the entire yard, with joyous sound.

"Oh, Dominic," she said, placing a hand on his arm. "Thank you from the bottom of my heart. I'll always treasure the memory of the look on Jason's face when he peered into that shopping bag. Did you see his eyes? They were actually sparkling. Thank you."

Dominic covered her hand with his own.

"You're welcome," he said, smiling. "It was my pleasure, believe me, although I'm thoroughly exhausted from trying to dress a human pogo stick. That is one charged-up little kid."

"That's a *happy* little kid because of your thoughtfulness."

Their smiles slowly faded as each became suddenly acutely aware of how close together they were on the swing, and of the feel of their hands meshed on Dominic's arm.

They looked directly into each other's eyes, not certain of what they saw there, not knowing what they *wished* to see.

Had seconds passed? Minutes? Neither knew. It was a moment out of time, with an otherworldly quality to it.

It had been Tessa who had broken the spell by pulling her hand and gaze free of Dominic's hold....

Dominic rolled onto his stomach in the rumpled bed, then shifted onto his back again in a restless surge of energy.

Face it, Bonelli, he told himself. He'd wanted to kiss Tessa. It had taken every ounce of willpower he possessed to not slide his hand to the nape of her neck, then capture her enticing lips with his.

Heat rocketed through him as he remembered that moment, as he recalled the white-hot desire that had consumed him.

Oh, yes, he'd wanted to kiss Tessa. He'd wanted to kiss, caress, explore every inch of her. He'd wanted to make love to her through the entire night.

And he didn't like the truth of that data, not one damn bit. Tessa and Jason had done tricky things to his mind and emotions. How and why they were capable of doing it, he didn't know. What he *was* certain of was that it wasn't going to happen again.

With a groan of fatigue, he finally drifted off to sleep.

And dreamed of Tessa.

On Thursday morning, Tessa stood in front of the stove stirring scrambled eggs in a frying pan. She pressed the fingertips of her free hand to her forehead, willing the nagging headache she'd awakened with to disappear.

Not a chance, she thought glumly. She'd gone to bed the night before with the headache, and it had still been there to greet her when she'd opened her eyes at dawn's light, just as it had been on Tuesday and Wednesday morning.

Well, what did she expect? When a person wasn't getting enough sleep night after night, the end result would be a fatigue-induced headache.

She was so angry at herself she could scream. The cause of her insomnia was perfectly clear to her, and it was ridiculous. She hadn't succumbed to such nonsense when she'd been an adolescent, and her behavior certainly wasn't becoming in a woman of nearly thirty years old.

"Absurd," she muttered, spooning the eggs onto two plates. "Silly. Disgusting. Asinine. And really, really dumb."

Her sleepless nights, damn the man, were caused by Dominic Bonelli.

She added bacon and toast to the plates, carried them to the table, then went to the bottom of the stairs.

"Jason," she called, "breakfast is ready. Lickety-split, kiddo. It's on the table."

"'Kay," Jason yelled. "Comin'."

Tessa returned to the kitchen, poured herself a cup of coffee, Jason a glass of milk, then sank onto a chair at the table with a weary sigh.

Dominic, her mind echoed. His unexpected visit of Monday evening had totally unsettled her. Every detail of the time spent with him on the porch kept repeating in her mental vision like a movie playing over and over.

She could see Dominic so clearly it was as though he were sitting across the table from her at that very moment. His aroma of soap, spicy after-shave and fresh air was there, as was the sound of his deep, masculine laughter.

She saw him nervous, endearingly unsure of himself, as he explained his purchase of the cowboy outfit for Jason. The beautiful image of Jason's small hand being held in Dominic's large and strong hand, haunted her with its poignancy.

And then? Dear heaven, something strange and sensual had happened when she and Dominic had looked into each other's eyes. She could still feel the heat that had thrummed through her body, and the increased tempo of her heart.

Dominic's dark, compelling eyes had held her immobile. She'd been so incredibly *aware* of him as a man, as well as experiencing a near-painful heightened acknowledgment of her own femininity. Her breasts had become heavy, aching for a soothing touch, and even her skin had tingled.

It had been unsettling, to say the least. She'd vowed years before to never again fall prey to a man's charm or masculine magnetism. The heartbreaking lesson she'd learned from her affair with Cliff had held her in good stead, enabling her to keep the occasional men she met at arm's length. *She* was in control of her feelings, emotions, her life.

Until now.

Until Dominic Bonelli.

"Oh, Tessa," she said, shaking her head.

Her slumbering womanliness was being awakened by the last man on earth she'd wish to have anything to do with. Well, she was going to put her femininity back to sleep, thank you very much. Somehow.

Tessa was pulled from her reverie as Jason came running into the room, then slid onto his chair.

She inwardly groaned as she once again saw the cowboy suit Dominic had given Jason, just as she had every morning since the child had received it. *That* was not helping her mental muddle one iota.

"Jason," she said, "you own other clothes, you know. You're going to wear that suit out."

"I love it, Mom," he said, beaming. "You washed it again for me, so I put it on."

"I had no choice but to wash it. You're a dusty, dirty cowpoke by the end of the day."

Jason frowned. "Are you mad at me 'cause I wore it again?"

"No, sweetheart," she said, smiling, "of course I'm not. I'm glad you like it, and you look wonderful in it."

"It's great," he said, then shoveled in a forkful of eggs.

Tessa forced herself to eat, hoping the nourishment would ease her headache at least a little.

"Dominic sure is nice," Jason said. "Right, Mom?"

"What? Oh, yes, it was very nice of him to give you such a marvelous surprise."

"Yep, but he's nice because he's my friend, too. I've never had a grown-up man as my friend before. He said he's my friend, so he is. That's cool."

"Yes," she said softly.

Oh, Jason, Jason. It was becoming painfully apparent that he missed having a male influence in his life. He'd never said a word on the subject, but his reaction to Dominic's offered friendship was speaking volumes. How shattering it would be to her son if he knew that his new hero was in actuality his father—and that Dominic refused to acknowledge that fact.

"I betcha Dominic will come to see me again," Jason said.

No! Tessa thought. She didn't want Dominic to come near her *or* Jason. Not *ever* again.

"Friends do that, you know," Jason rambled on. "They visit each other. I could show him how high I can go on the swing in the play yard."

"Honey, Dominic is a very busy man. You mustn't count on his having time to spend here."

"He'll come to see me," Jason said. "I know he will." He paused. "Is he your friend, too? Did you shake hands and stuff? That would be good, Mom, 'cause then he could visit you, too. Neato."

"Jason, please don't expect Dominic to visit. I don't want you to be disappointed or sad."

"Will *you* be sad if he doesn't come see us?"

"No."

"Don't you like him?"

"Jason, eat your breakfast. The kids will start arriving any minute now, and you know I like to have the kitchen cleaned up before they get here."

"Mommy, don't you like Dominic?"

Tessa sighed. "Yes, okay, I like Dominic."

"Good."

"Eat."

"Yep. I'm going to grow up to be as big and tall as Dominic is, and have muscles like him." He took a bite of toast.

Oh, Lord, spare me, Tessa thought. Everything was getting so out of control. It was a nightmare, all of it.

A knock at the front door brought Tessa to her feet.

"Chew," she said to Jason as she left the kitchen.

As she crossed the living room, she could see a man beyond the screen door.

"Hi," he said, when she got to the door. "I'm Joe Bonelli."

Why not? Tessa thought dryly. Heaven forbid she should miss out on meeting one of the Bonelli brothers. This one, too, looked like the others. And this one, too, drat it all, wasn't quite as tall, or handsome, or as well built as Dominic.

"What can I do for you, Joe?" she said, managing a small smile.

"I'm plumbing. The others will be along soon to finish up the roof today. I'm going to start on your plumbing problems. Nothing major is wrong. You've just got some rusty pipes that I'm going to replace. It won't cause you any inconvenience. Well, not a lot, anyway. Jeff's report says you have turn-offs by each unit, so I won't have to shut down the water to the entire house."

"Whatever," she said, throwing up her hands in a gesture of submission. "Make yourself at home, Joe." She unlatched the screen. "I'd appreciate your letting me know where you'll be working at what time, so I can reroute the children to another bathroom."

"Sure thing."

"Oh, and I need the kitchen operational at the lunch hour."

Jason came running into the room.

"Dominic?" he yelled, racing to the door. He stopped and frowned. "Oh, I thought I heard Dominic."

Joe smiled at him through the screen. "Nope. I'm Joe. People get the Bonelli boys mixed up all the time. You know Dom?"

"Dominic is my friend," Jason said, puffing out his chest. "We shook hands and said we'd be friends. He gave me this cowboy suit."

Joe's eyes widened. "Dom . . . Dominic Bonelli, my brother . . . gave you that outfit?"

"Yep."

Wake up, Tessa, she told herself. She was supposed to keep Jason away from any one-on-one contact with Dominic's brothers. Those had been His Majesty's orders.

"Jason, please go carry your plate to the sink," she said.

"I did."

"Oh."

"When did Dom give you that outfit?" Joe asked Jason.

"The other night," Jason said, "when he came to visit. He sat on the porch swing with my mom while I was riding my broom horse, and they talked a lot, and she just told me that she likes him, and—"

"Jason," Tessa interrupted, feeling a warm flush on her cheeks, "Joe has to get to work on the plumbing now. Oh, look, here comes Jeremiah."

"Dom actually sat on that swing?" Joe said, pointing to it. "Just chilled-out, laid-back and relaxed? Dominic Bonelli?"

Tessa rolled her eyes heavenward. "We're not talking about a major miracle here."

"But close," Joe said, chuckling. "Very close. Dom doesn't do leisure time. He just works, works, works." He looked at the swing, Tessa, then slid his gaze over Jason's outfit. "This is interesting. Very, *very* interesting."

Before Tessa could think of anything to say to defuse Joe's obviously busy mind, Jeremiah hit the front porch with a bounce, and a yelp of glee at seeing Jason.

The day at Rainbow's End had officially begun.

Tessa pressed one hand to her forehead in a silent plea to her headache to vanish, then mentally counted off the hours left until the day ahead would be blessedly over.

Chapter Nine

Murphy's Law, Tessa decided in the late afternoon, was working overtime at Rainbow's End. Everything that could have gone wrong that day, had gone wrong, with a few extras thrown in for good measure.

There had not been any major crises, just an ongoing series of little upsets that had increased the intensity of Tessa's headache and the frazzled state of her nerves.

Two of the children had suffered slightly skinned knees in the play yard, resulting in sonic-boom volume levels of wails, and the need for Mickey Mouse bandages and lots of hugs.

Jeremiah had no sooner finished eating his lunch then he upchucked it onto the kitchen floor. The pale little boy had been tucked beneath a fluffy blanket on the cot in Tessa's office, where he promptly fell asleep.

A wheel had been broken off a plastic truck; a tug-of-war between two girls had amputated an arm and a leg from a doll; and Jason had spilled orange juice down the front of his western shirt.

To add to all the confusion, Joe had seemed to be constantly in the wrong place at the worst time.

When Patty started singing "Happy Days Are Here Again" at the top of her lungs, Tessa shot her a look that could have curdled milk.

"Oops," Patty said, laughing. "I was just trying to cheer things up around here. Has this been a day, or has this been a day?"

"This has been a day," Tessa said with a sigh, "*not* to remember. I just checked on Jeremiah again. He's awake, but is content to stay put. He's sure feeling punk, the poor little guy."

"Did you call his mother?"

"Yes, right after he redistributed his lunch. I told her I'd keep him quiet, and she said she'd try to leave work early, if possible, to come pick him up, but I guess she has a heartless boss. There's no telling what nasty bug Jeremiah has that he's no doubt shared with the others."

"Time will tell," Patty said in a singsong voice. "Ah, I hear a car. The mighty moms are beginning to arrive. This day is nearly history, Tessa."

"Amen," she said wearily.

"Tessa," a whiny voice said, "I gots polka dots on my tummy."

"Oh, good grief," she said.

She hurried across the kitchen to where Jeremiah stood in the doorway of the office. Joe passed her on his way to the kitchen sink. She knelt in front of Jeremiah and lifted his shirt.

"Chicken pox," she said with a moan. "Oh, sweetheart, you've got a full-blown case of chicken pox."

Jeremiah burst into tears. "I don't wanna be a chicken. I'm a boy. Don't make me be a chicken, Tessa."

Tessa scooped him up and settled onto a chair by the table, holding him on her lap.

"You're not going to turn into a chicken, Jeremiah. I promise you won't. That's just the silly name someone gave those kinds of spots on your tummy. You'll stay a boy, honest you will."

"Guaranteed," Joe said, looking over at them. "Hey, Jeremiah, chicken pox are cool. Your mom will put pink lotion on you, and you'll look like a birthday cake. No foolin', my two kids had chicken pox last year and they looked good enough to eat."

"Really?" Jeremiah said, dashing the tears from his cheeks. He pulled up his shirt to peer at his tummy. "A birthday cake?"

"Yep," Joe said, then his head and shoulders disappeared under the kitchen sink.

"Thank you, Joe," Tessa said to the general direction of his rear end.

"No problem," came a muffled reply.

The next forty-five minutes was a bustle of activity. Each mother that arrived to collect her child was informed that their darling had been exposed to chicken pox. Tessa passed out the sheets given to her by the health department regarding the disease. Reactions were varied, depending on whether their son or daughter had already suffered through the miserable, itchy, childhood malady.

Jason, Tessa thought glumly, had *not* had chicken pox. Jason was *going* to get chicken pox in approximately two to three weeks. *She* was not in the mood to have Jason get chicken pox. Darn and damn.

The last child had been picked up, Emma and Patty waved rather listless farewells and Tessa sighed with relief. In the next moment, she frowned and glanced quickly around the main room.

Where was Jason? she wondered, hurrying toward the kitchen.

Once there, she stopped in her tracks. Jason's small bottom was poking in the air next to Joe's larger one, their upper halves under the sink.

Great, she thought. She was supposed to keep Jason away from the Bonelli brothers. Well, tough. She was exhausted and needed five minutes to catch her breath. If Joe didn't mind having Jason in the way under the sink, so be it.

She sank onto a chair at the table, propped up her elbows and massaged her aching temples.

"Whoa!" Joe yelled suddenly.

"Yeow!" Jason hollered.

"Oh, good Lord," Tessa said, jumping to her feet.

Water sprayed from beneath the sink as Jason and Joe scrambled backward, soaking wet. Joe dived back under the sink and the water stopped shooting out over the kitchen.

"Whew," Joe said. "The turn-off knob was stripped. It held for a bit, then let go. Are you okay, Jason? The water was cold, and we sure are wet, aren't we, pal?"

Tessa's horrified gaze swept over the dripping wet stove, refrigerator, cupboards and floor.

"Wet," was all she managed to say.

"I'll clean it up," Joe said. "Don't worry about a thing."

"Whatever," she said, sinking back onto the chair. "That's one way to get Jason's cowboy suit clean." She paused. "I think I'm hysterical."

"That was pretty scary," Jason said, smiling, "but I'm a brave cowboy."

"You betcha," Joe said. He whipped a huge calico-print handkerchief out of his back pocket. "This is dry. We're in business."

As Joe dried Jason's face, then began to ruffle the boy's wet hair with the handkerchief, resulting in Jason's giggling in delight, it slowly dawned on Tessa what was taking place.

No! her mind screamed. He mustn't tousle Jason's hair. *Joe Bonelli must not see Jason's right ear!*

She got to her feet, feeling as though she were moving in slow motion, the pair on the floor seeming a mile away. Her demand that Joe stop what he was doing caught in her throat, with only a near sob escaping her lips.

"This isn't all bad, you know," Joe was saying to Jason. "When your mom tells you to hit the tub tonight, you can tell her you already had a bath *and* your hair washed. Your hair sure is soaked, though. I think we're going to need..." His voice trailed off and his hands stilled in midair. "A towel."

Joe's head snapped up and his eyes collided with Tessa's. She was standing ramrod-stiff, trembling fingertips pressed to her lips.

One second ticked into two, three, then four.

"Somethin' the matter, Joe?" Jason said.

"What?" Joe tore his gaze from Tessa's and looked at Jason. "No. No, nothing is wrong. This handkerchief just isn't big enough to get the job done, that's all." He got to his feet, and Jason scrambled to his. "You go on upstairs, dry off and change your clothes on your own. Hit the trail, cowboy."

"Yep." Jason ran from the room.

Joe ripped a paper towel from the roll in the holder mounted beneath a cupboard. He dragged the paper over his wet face, wadded the paper into a tight ball, then looked at Tessa, no hint of a smile on his face.

"What in the hell is going on here?" he said.

"I...I don't know what you mean," Tessa said, her voice unsteady.

Joe flung the paper towel into the sink.

"Knock it off, Tessa," he said, a rough edge to his voice. "Your son is a Bonelli. There's no mistaking the Bonelli ear. I saw it, the little nitch in Jason's right ear. I also now realize that he looks just like my son did at that age. Hell, like *I* looked at five years old, like all the Bonelli males looked as young boys. I didn't catch it at first because I wasn't thinking along those lines. But now? That kid's father is a Bonelli."

"Oh, God," Tessa whispered. She sank back onto the chair as her legs refused to hold her for another instant.

Joe crossed the room and gripped the top of another chair, leaning slightly forward.

"Talk to me," he said, "or I'll be forced to draw my own conclusions."

Tessa shook her head.

"Damn it." He straightened and shoved his hands through his wet hair. "Okay, we'll do this your way. Actually, it's clear as a bell. Dom isn't the executor of some screwy will that says he's to oversee how your inheritance is spent. *He's* paying for this work on your house because he's Jason's father.

"You and Dom had a fling, or affair, or whatever, about six years ago, and the result was Jason. What I can't figure out is why you waited all this time to tell Dom he has a son. It's obvious he didn't know until now, because he wouldn't have stood by and allowed his son to live in a place that was falling apart. Dom is really big on responsibility."

"You don't understand."

"You've got that straight. I don't know what your game is. I'm not real thrilled with Dominic at the moment, either. He apparently didn't intend for the family to know about his son. That stinks. Jason is a Bonelli, just like the rest of us. We have the right to know that he exists. Bonellis are Bonellis, all of us, no matter what."

"Joe..."

"I'll clean up your kitchen," he said, turning and starting back toward the sink. "Then I'm going to round up the family, and we're all going to have a little chat with Dom."

Tessa jumped to her feet. "No. Joe, please, no, don't do that. I promised Dominic that I'd keep Jason away from you and your brothers while you were working here. You mustn't tell him what you've discovered. Oh, Joe, please, listen to me. This is far more complicated than you think. Leave it alone. *Please, Joe, leave it alone.*"

He turned to look at her, his voice quiet and gentle when he spoke again.

"I can't do that, Tessa. We are an old-fashioned, close-knit family. We have a code of honor that must be followed to enable us to be true to who we are, what we stand for and believe in.

"Dom is breaking the rules. He's accustomed to being in charge, since he's the head of the family. But this time, by God, he's out of line and he's accountable for that."

"Joe, please, think about Jason. He's just an innocent child. He doesn't deserve to have his world turned upside down."

"I *am* thinking about Jason," he said, splaying out one hand on his chest. "What he deserves is to have what's due him as a Bonelli. Jason has a grandmother with enough love in her heart for a million kids. He has aunts, uncles and cousins. He has a big family, Tessa, that will be there for him through good times and bad.

"And do you know what else? You're Jason's mother, and that means the family is yours, too. I don't give a tinker's damn what Dom says about that. You and Jason are part of us, all of us. I've never before crossed swords with Dom, none of us have, but there's a first time for everything."

"But I'm *not* Jason's mother." She sat back down, covered her face with her hands and shook her head. "This is a nightmare. I just want to be left alone with my son to raise him, love him, as I've always done. We were doing fine, just the two of us. He's Jason Robert Russell, my baby." A sob caught in her throat. "I wish I'd never heard of the Bonellis, any of you."

"I'm sorry I upset you. But I don't understand. One minute you're saying you're not Jason's mother, the next second you're calling him your son. You're not going to start crying, are you?"

Tessa dropped her hands and glared at him.

"A crying jag is not going to solve this, Joe Bonelli. What will, is your keeping your damn mouth shut. I don't give a hoot in hell about your Bonelli code of honor. I have a voice in this matter, mister. I intend to protect my son from you, all of you. Get out of my house." She got to her feet. *"Now!"*

"Whew," Joe said, grinning at her. "You're really something when you get on a rip. I do believe, ma'am, that Dominic Bonelli has met his match."

"Mom," Jason called, running into the kitchen. "Will you help me get my boots back on? They didn't get wet."

"What's the magic word, sport?" Joe said.

"Please," Jason said.

"That's the one," Joe said, nodding. "That's the magic word for my kids, too." He looked directly at Tessa. "For *all* the Bonellis, as a matter of fact."

"Joe . . ."

"I have to do what I have to do, Tessa," he said. "I'm sorry."

"Mom? Joe?" Jason said, his eyes darting back and forth between them. "What's wrong? Mommy?"

"Nothing, sweetheart," she said, managing a small smile. "I'll help you with your boots. There's nothing wrong, Jason."

"No, Jason, nothing is wrong," Joe said. "Things that are long overdue are going to be set to rights."

Several hours later, Tessa sat on the swing on the front porch, willing the tranquillity of the peaceful desert night to ease her inner turmoil.

The evening was a blur in her mind, the activities and conversations shared with Jason having been performed by rote.

She'd gone to bed an hour after Jason had been read a story and tucked in, but despite her bone-weary fatigue, she had been unable to sleep.

Her world was falling apart, and everything she held dear was being threatened. Despite the vow she'd made years before to be in charge of her life, that control was slipping through her hands like grains of sand.

Miles away, somewhere in the city, the Bonellis were no doubt having a family meeting, and Dominic was probably being confronted with the fact that the existence of his son had been discovered.

Dear heaven, what was going to happen?

If forced to acknowledge Jason as his, would Dominic then seek custody of his son?

Was she going to lose her beloved Jason?

Chapter Ten

Dominic glanced at his watch, then pressed harder on the gas pedal. The traffic was heavy, and a moment later he was forced to reduce his speed again. He swore under his breath, then mentally ordered himself to relax.

A family meeting, he thought, frowning. It had been a couple of years since one of these had been organized. There'd been a stretch of time when the family had gathered regularly: formulating plans for Bonelli Painting and Restoration, seeing to the proper training of his brothers, arranging loans to enable the business to be launched.

There had been meetings called, he remembered, by his sisters, as well, as they made decisions regarding their futures. Carmen had requested and received a loan to attend art school. About a year later, Maria had rallied the troops to announce that she was getting married and planned to have a dozen babies.

So now what? he wondered. Everyone and everything was under control, as far as he knew. His brothers' business was thriving, Carmen was getting ongoing excellent reviews on her oil paintings and Maria was happily expecting her third child.

Was someone ill? Did his brothers want to expand their business even more, perhaps by purchasing additional vehicles or equipment? If a new house or car was being contemplated, it didn't take a family meeting to discuss it.

Hell, he didn't know what was on the agenda. What he *was* aware of was that he wasn't in the mood for this. He'd had a grueling day, was rushing to his mother's house directly from the office and he was starving. He wanted his dinner.

Joe had left a message with Gladys regarding the family meeting to be held that night at seven o'clock at, as per tradition, their mother's house. He had not, the secretary had related, asked to speak directly with Dominic.

Whatever, he thought with a mental shrug. He knew from experience that the person telephoning wasn't necessarily the one who'd requested the gathering. Usually, though, several days' notice was given. But not this time. Well, this had better be important, that was for damn sure.

Dominic's frown and clenched jaw disappeared as he left the busy main road and drove slowly through the exclusive neighborhood where his mother now lived.

Knowing that she had the lovely, large home that she deserved never failed to bring him a sense of inner eace. It had been a long hard journey from the poverty of his youth to the quality of life his family now enjoyed. It was his responsibility to care for his family, and he was satisfied with what he had accomplished thus far.

He turned at one more corner, then pulled in next to the last of the many vehicles parked in front of the big two-story house.

Entering without knocking, he went down the Spanish-tiled entry hall to the sunken living room off to the left. As he entered the room, the buzz of conversation stopped, and all eyes were on him.

"Hello," he said, pulling the knot of his tie down several inches. "No kids? You all got baby-sitters on short notice." He crossed the room and dropped a kiss on his mother's cheek. "Hi, beautiful. How's my best girl in the whole world?"

"You look tired, Dom," Delores Bonelli said, scrutinizing his face.

She was short, plump and wore her salt-and-pepper hair in a bun at the nape of her neck. When she smiled, her eyes danced with merriment.

"I'm beat," Dominic said. He swept his gaze over the group, noting that everyone was there—husbands, wives, the entire family. And not one of them was smiling. "So? What's up? Who called for this?"

Joe got to his feet. "*I* did."

Dominic sat down in a high-backed leather chair, slouched a bit, undid the two top buttons on his shirt, then laced his fingers loosely on his chest.

"Okay, Joe," he said. "Go for it."

Joe took a deep breath, cleared his throat, then squared his shoulders.

"Everyone knows why we're here," he said. "
thought it best to allow a bit of time to digest this."

"Everyone except me," Dominic said. "Gladys sai
you didn't even ask to speak to me. Is there a reaso
for that, Joe?"

"I didn't want to get into this with you on th
phone. It's too important, Dom."

"Well, you all look like you've come from a fu
neral," Dominic said. "Spit it out, Joe. What's th
subject matter of this meeting?"

"Jason Robert Russell," Joe said quietly. "Jaso
Robert Russell . . . Bonelli."

Dominic lunged to his feet so quickly that Joe too
a step backward.

"Are you out of your mind?" Dominic said,
steely edge to his voice. His eyes darted around th
room, then centered on Joe again. "Do you realiz
what you're doing?"

"Yes," Joe said, then forced more strength into hi
voice. "Yes, I know exactly what I'm doing. It's lon
overdue, but I'm acknowledging the truth. Jaso
Russell is a Bonelli."

"The truth? At what cost?" Dominic roared. H
swept one arm through the air. "Which family in thi
room do you plan to destroy, Joe?" He laughed, bu
it was a short, humorless bark of sound. "Well, on
thing is clear. It wasn't you who... You're an idiot, bu
not a complete fool, I guess. This is really a rotten sho
you're pulling on Vince, Benny or Frank."

"Now wait a minute, Dom," Joe said.

"What's wrong with you guys?" Dominic raged, a
though Joe hadn't spoken. "Joe said you all kne
what this meeting was about. Why didn't one of yo
stop him? More precisely, the man who's responsibl

or this mess should never have allowed this meeting o take place.''

"The man responsible didn't know what the meeting was about, damn it," Joe yelled.

"What in the hell are you saying, Joe?" Dominic snapped.

"Come off it, Dom," Joe said. "You're so used to being in charge you've begun to believe you can change facts to suit you.

"Well, not this time, big brother. You're not going to pretend that Jason doesn't exist. Fixing up the house where he lives isn't enough, not even close. He deserves to be part of this family, and so does his mother, Tessa. And that, Dominic, is the way it's going to be.''

Dominic narrowed his eyes and looked at each of his brothers in turn.

"Very clever," he said coldly. "You got together and planned a 'safety in numbers' routine. You're all trying to protect your marriages." He nodded. "Nice try, but I was with you in Las Vegas, remember? I assume you know that's where Jason was conceived, during the celebration of the opening of my firm.

"Tessa, by the way, is Jason's *aunt,* not his mother, although the boy doesn't know that. Oh, you celebrated big time, drank like there was no tomorrow. One of you picked up Janice Russell and went to bed with her. I was keeping Jason's existence a secret to protect whichever one of you it was so your marriage wouldn't be in jeopardy. I made Jason *my* responsibility.''

"With just cause, Dom," Joe said quietly. "Jason is *your* son.''

"Ah, hell, that's enough of this garbage," Dominic said, starting across the room. "I'm tired and I'm not playing this game."

"It's no game, Dom," Frank said. "You're Jason's father."

Dominic stopped and spun around. "Don't push me, Frank. I know you guys are trying to protect what you have but you can't use me to do it."

"Shut up," Frank said. He got to his feet and crossed the room to stand directly in front of Dominic. "For once in your life, just shut the hell up and listen."

"Good Lord," Carmen muttered. "Frankie has a death wish."

"Jason was conceived in Las Vegas? Then that really cinches it," Frank said. "Yeah, we drank in Vegas, but so did you, Dom. We all saw you relax, actually unbend, become...become human. It was good to see. You're always so closed, always thinking, thinking, thinking about your responsibilities. But that weekend? Man, you kicked back and went with it. We were topping off your drinks, Dom. You were totally smashed."

"What?" Dominic said, his voice a hoarse whisper. "You topped off my drinks?"

"We didn't do it *to* you," Frank went on. "We did it *for* you. You'd worked so hard for all of us. You deserved to have a great time. When the party girl approached you, we figured, hell, why not? This is Dom's celebration. Let him do what he wants. *You* spent the night with the woman, Dominic. It wasn't one of us. It was you, I swear to God it was. *Jason Russell is your son!*"

Mental images never before seen, slammed against Dominic's mind like hammering blows.

A tall, slender woman hanging on his arm, whispering in his ear... a glass of liquor that was never empty... drinking, drinking... a room, a bed, the woman laughing, beckoning him to the erotic round bed... talking, telling her that money was power, money was the key to the door of success, of having finally made it big... then falling into an abyss of dark, dreamless sleep...

Dominic dragged both hands down his face.

"My God," he whispered, "I didn't remember." He shook his head in an attempt to shake away the haunting pictures. "I really thought that one of you guys had..." He stopped speaking and stared up at the ceiling.

Jason was his son, he thought incredulously. *His.* That funny little kid, who had nearly popped a seam because he was so excited about having a cowboy suit, was his son. That boy, who had looked at him with such innocence, so vulnerable and trusting, and asked if Dominic was his friend, was his child, born of his seed.

Dominic shifted his gaze to his right hand, staring at it, remembering the feel of Jason's small hand in his. Then he suddenly saw Tessa's smile, heard her say that he was now officially a Bonelli who was warm and friendly.

No one in the room spoke. All eyes were on Dominic. Frank and Joe returned to their seats, each reaching for their wife's hand.

Dominic dropped his hand to his side, his eyes darting around the room.

Damn it, he fumed inwardly. He felt as though he were on trial and being stripped bare by judgments passed on him by a family *he* was the head of. What was next? They'd give him a list of *their* instructions regarding what he should do about Jason Russell? Not in this lifetime. He was in charge here.

"I'm leaving now," he said gruffly. "Good night, family."

"Dom," Delores said.

"Yes?" he said, looking at his mother.

"This woman in Las Vegas," she said. "Where is she now?"

"She died," Dominic said wearily, suddenly thoroughly exhausted. "Her sister, Tessa, has raised Jason alone from the day he was born. He's five years old."

"How is it," Delores said, "that you only now know he exists?"

"I received a legal file in the mail. I guess there was a snafu when the office of the attorney who handled the whole thing was closed after he passed away. I thought at first that Tessa was pulling a scam, but I've since concluded that isn't true.

"I'd like to know, though, Joe, how *you* suddenly came to be aware that Jason was a Bonelli."

"It was a fluke," Joe said, "so don't blame Tessa. Jason got wet and I was drying his face and hair. She asked me . . . hell, she begged me . . . not to pursue this when I discovered Jason's identity. I told her I couldn't do that."

"You saw his ear," Dominic said, sighing.

"Yeah, Dom, I saw it, and I knew. I also realized that you intended to keep Jason's existence a secret, and I couldn't stand by and allow that to happen."

"Dom," his mother said gently, "do you believe that this child is yours?"

Dominic sighed again. "Yes, I guess so. Yes, all right, he's mine." He narrowed his eyes. "He's *my* responsibility. I'm already seeing to his needs and doing what has to be done. I'm having the house repaired, I'll set up a trust fund for his education, I'll convince Tessa to accept monthly support money. End of story."

"Tessa Russell sounds like a strong, courageous woman," Delores said. "She has raised her sister's child as though he were her own, and she's done it all alone. Is that correct? There's no other family?"

"No, no family," Dominic said. "Tessa will have it easier from here on out because I'll provide the money to make that possible. There's no more to be said on the subject. This meeting is over."

Delores got to her feet. "No, Dom, this family meeting is *not* over, and you are not leaving yet."

A collective gasp went up from the group, then a heavy silence fell over the room as mother and eldest son stared at each other.

Delores lifted her chin. "You have been the head of this family for many, many years, Dom. It broke my heart to see such a young boy take on so many responsibilities, but I had no choice other than to let you do it. I had little ones to care for, and with your father gone, I turned to you.

"All of us have leaned on you through the years, looked to you for guidance, for strength, direction. You were forced into the role of a man and were robbed of your childhood. I'll always regret that, yet be grateful for what you've done."

"Mother—"

"No, Dom, hear me out. We have never questioned your role as the head of the Bonelli family. Never. Your word was law, your decisions final and you've provided well for all of us."

"Your point?" Dominic said, a muscle jumping in his jaw.

"My point, my son," Delores said, lifting her chin another notch, "is that this time you are wrong. This time, things are not going to be done the way you decree. This time *I* am making decisions and *I'm* in charge."

"I don't believe this," Carmen said.

"Shh," Maria said. "Oh, dear heaven, I don't believe this, either."

"Shh," Maria's husband said.

"I don't mean to be rude, Mother," Dominic said tightly, "but—"

"Then don't be," Delores interrupted. "Just listen. Dominic, you have a son. It's not enough that you give him money, a fine home, an education. Yes, as his father, those things are your responsibility to provide, but what of love, Dominic? Responsibility doesn't equal love. Money isn't love.

"I fear for you, Dom, for what's in your heart, your mind, your very soul. Even more, what *isn't* there. Have we done this to you by leaning on you so heavily all these years? Are we the cause of your not knowing the difference between love and responsibility? Dear God, forgive me if that's true."

"That's enough," Dominic said. "I'm not on trial here. I've provided for all of you the way my father would have wanted me to. You've got no complaints, any of you. I'll see to Jason's needs, too. He's my *re-*

sponsibility and I don't want, nor will I tolerate, in-
terference from any of you. Is that clear?"

"Dominic," Delores said, "Jason is my grandson.
Tessa, in my mind, is his mother. They're part of this
family, and welcome in my home. I intend to hug Jason to my breast, just as I do all my grandchildren.
Tessa and Jason will eat at my table, share in the lives
and love of all the Bonellis because they *are* Bonellis."

"Damn it, you have no right to—"

"I have every right. *I* am the mother of this family.
You may see yourself as the one in charge of responsibility, but *I* am in charge of family love. Tessa and
Jason will have what they deserve from our hearts.
None of us will tell Jason that you are his father. That
is for you and Tessa to work out. We'll have another
explanation for the little one as to where we all came
from, if that's what you want."

"I have no intention of informing Jason Robert
Russell that he's my son!"

"So be it," Delores said. "We'll respect that decision."

"Thanks a helluva lot," he said, his tone sarcastic.
"You're letting me know that Tessa and Jason will be
here at family celebrations, having a grand old time.
The hell with how I might feel about *that*. Well, go for
it, family. Include them in everything, for all I care.
But count *me* out. I'm not going to interact with them
because I was told to at a family meeting. Not a
chance. You don't dictate to me. Not ever."

Dominic turned and strode from the room. A few
moments later, everyone cringed as the front door
slammed.

Chapter Eleven

No news, Tessa decided on Sunday morning, is not always good news. Silence is *not* always golden—and whatever other clichés might be available to misapply to the nerve-racking situation, Tessa added.

She'd had a telephone call on Friday morning from the secretary at Bonelli Painting and Restoration informing her that the roof and plumbing projects were completed at Rainbow's End. The men were scheduled to be on another job that day, but would return on Monday to begin work on the outside of the house.

"Oh? Just what exactly are they going to do to it?" Tessa had asked.

"You don't know?" the secretary said.

"Not really." Tessa paused. "The woman is always the last to know." She sighed dramatically, then rolled her eyes in self-disgust. "Forget it. Do you have even hint of what they plan to do to the outside of the house?''

"Sure. I'm looking at the work order. They'll scrape off all the old paint, then put on fresh paint. Great, huh? There's a note here that says you're to pick the color you want."

"Really? How nice," Tessa said dryly. "Well, I think I'll have it done in multicolored stripes. I mean, geez, this *is* Rainbow's End. Why not have a house that looks like a rainbow? Good idea, don't you think?"

"Well...um...yes, that sounds...interesting. You bet. Whatever you want, Ms. Russell. Shall I write that on the work order?"

"No! Good grief, I was kidding. I'll think about the color. Okay?"

"Super idea. You think about it. The guys will show you sample charts so you can choose what will look the best. Bye for now."

"Bye," she'd said wearily.

As she replaced the receiver, she'd continued an imaginary conversation with the secretary.

Say, honey bun, you didn't happen to hear what went on at the Bonelli family meeting, did you? Is Dominic planning to murder me? Did he shoot any of his brothers? Did his brothers shoot him? Should I snatch up my son and leave town?

"Tessa Russell," she said aloud, "you're definitely losing it."

By early afternoon on Sunday, she was toying with the idea of taking Jason into town, when Jeremiah's mother called and asked if Jason could come play. Since Jason had already been exposed to the chicken pox, would Tessa allow him to spend the afternoon and evening with a very bored Jeremiah?

Jason thought the idea was "cool," and a polka-dot Jeremiah and his mother drove out to pick him up. Jason was, of course, wearing his cowboy suit.

Tessa wandered aimlessly around the house, scolded herself with a cliché about idle hands, which she couldn't remember in its entirety, then settled behind her desk in the small office to get caught up on the paperwork for Rainbow's End.

She really enjoyed the accounting side of the day-care center, she mused. There was a satisfying orderliness about the ledger and a mental hooray when the columns balanced. How wonderful it would be if she could so easily bring her life back under her command.

Just after four o'clock, the telephone on the desk rang, and she jerked in surprise as the shrill sound shattered the silence in the small room. She picked up the receiver halfway through the second ring.

"Hello?"

"It's Dominic. I'd like to come out there and talk to you."

No! "Yes, all right. When?" *Never!*

"I'm leaving now. Goodbye."

The dial tone buzzed in her ear before she could echo Dominic's goodbye, and she replaced the receiver slowly, realizing her hand was trembling.

This is it, she thought, getting to her feet.

She hadn't been able to gauge Dominic's mood from the extremely brief call, but she was certain that Joe had followed through on his plan to have a family meeting. So Dominic had been confronted with Jason's existence. Had he been forced to acknowledge what she already knew, that Jason was *his* son?

Yes, of course, he had, because his brothers would stand united with the truth: it had been Dominic who had gone off with Janice in Las Vegas.

Would Dominic tell *her* that he was Jason's father? Or would he attempt to continue the charade of stating that one of his brothers was responsible for Jason's conception?

He'd had many hours since that gathering on Thursday night to formulate a plan of action regarding his son. He held in his hands the power to control her entire future happiness.

"Damn it, no," she said.

This wasn't going to happen to her again. She was *not* going to be treated like a marionette whose strings were being maneuvered by someone other than herself. She'd been dictated to too many times in her life by outside forces.

Well, not this time, by heaven.

Tessa stomped up the stairs, combed her hair, freshened her lipstick and tucked a bright blue cotton blouse into her jeans.

She settled onto the swing on the porch, narrowed her eyes, pursed her lips and waited for Dominic Bonelli.

As Dominic drove toward Rainbow's End, he was aware of his bone-deep fatigue. It had been so long since he'd had an energy-restoring solid night's sleep, he'd forgotten what one felt like.

He hadn't seen, nor spoken to, any member of his family since the meeting Thursday night. He'd had no desire to communicate with them, and no Bonelli had left any messages for him with Gladys, or on his answering machine at home. So be it.

He'd needed the time to think, to digest what he'd learned from his brothers and to contemplate his options regarding the fact that Jason Robert Russell was his son.

Dear God, Jason was his son.

That truth had hammered against his brain unmercifully. *Jason was his son.* He'd struggled unsuccessfully to move past that echoing message, to get in touch with himself to discover exactly how he felt about it.

But his mind refused to travel forward. It simply repeated over and over that Jason was his son.

Why was he going to Rainbow's End? Hell, he didn't know. He'd been pacing his living room like a caged lion for hours, then had snatched up the receiver to the telephone on impulse and called Tessa.

He was, he supposed, hoping that by seeing Tessa and Jason, he would feel centered again. The emotional isolation he'd felt since leaving his mother's house had created the sensation of being the only person on earth, alone with his tangled thoughts.

So, yes, all right, he was, perhaps, running to a woman for comfort, which was not a welcome realization, but at least Tessa would never know.

Seeing her, the boy, the house, would reaffirm his sense of responsibility, get him back on the right track.

The boy.

Jason.

His son.

"Damn it," he said, smacking the steering wheel with the palm of his hand.

He didn't *want* a son. Or a wife. He'd been the head of the Bonelli family for years, and now enjoyed and protected his freedom. His role in Jason's life would go no further than his providing for the child's material needs.

Responsibility doesn't equal love. Money isn't love.

Delores's words suddenly slammed against Dominic's mind.

Are we the cause of your not knowing the difference between love and responsibility? Dear God, forgive me if that's true.

His mother, he reasoned, was endearingly naive and saw hugs and kisses as the solution to all that might be wrong.

Even though Delores Bonelli had suffered through years of poverty after her husband's death, she had still managed to emerge from that era wearing rose-colored glasses with which to view the world. She simply didn't understand the intensity of the responsibility that Dominic had taken on, he decided.

Responsibility doesn't equal love. Money isn't love.

Dominic shook his head.

Delores was operating on a different plane than he was. What would have become of them all if he hadn't been willing to step in and take charge of the family? He didn't expect a brass band and flowery testimonials for his deeds. He'd done what was needed at the time, pure and simple.

But he sure as hell wasn't going to start questioning himself, his values, his mode of conduct now that everyone was provided for and things were running smoothly.

As much as he sincerely loved his mother, he felt that she had no right to use her definition of love as a measuring stick against his. No.

If Delores intended to welcome Tessa and Jason into the Bonelli family, so be it. *He* wasn't having any part of that. He would see to Jason's financial and material welfare. He would meet his responsibility for the boy head-on.

His son.

"Ah, hell," Dominic said aloud.

He gripped the steering wheel more tightly, pressed harder on the gas pedal and scowled.

By the time Tessa saw the billowing dust in the distance from Dominic's approaching car, she'd worked herself into a frenzied combination of anger and fear.

She was furious at the loss of control over her life.

She was terrified that Dominic was coming to announce that he planned to seek custody of Jason.

When Dominic parked in front of the house, then started up the front walkway, she absently registered the fact that he looked fantastic in dark slacks and a yellow dress shirt open at the neck.

She got to her feet, and as he stepped onto the porch, she curled her hands into tight fists at her sides.

"Hello, Tessa," Dominic said, not smiling. "I came here to—"

"Dominic," she interrupted, "I did the best I could keeping Jason away from your brothers while they were working here. Therefore I refuse to apologize for what happened with Jason and Joe. It just happened, that's all.

"I don't know what took place at the family meeting Joe intended to organize, and I don't really care.

Why? Because no matter what was divulged during that gathering, the fact remains that Jason is my son. *Mine*."

"Tessa—"

"Shut up. You denied being Jason's father from the onset and tried to dump the whole business on one of your brothers. That stinks, Bonelli, it really does. You don't deserve Jason. You refused to acknowledge the fact that he's yours. Well, he's *not* yours, he's mine, and I'll fight you with everything I have—"

Sudden tears filled Tessa's eyes and her voice began to tremble.

"I won't let you have my baby. I won't. I won't." A sob caught in her throat.

"Ah, Tessa," Dominic said.

Before he realized he had done it, he reached for her, pulling her into his arms, holding her close.

And Tessa cried.

She wrapped her arms around Dominic, splaying her hands across his back, buried her face in his shirt and wept. The emotions that had been tormenting her had been too overwhelming, for too long. She was exhausted in mind and body, and to her, Dominic felt strong, powerful and solid, a safe haven where she could rest.

And so she cried.

Dominic tightened his hold on Tessa even more, feeling her pain as though it were his own, her sobs causing his heart to ache for her. His need to comfort, soothe, assure her that all was well, was like nothing he'd experienced before.

He wanted to slay the foe that was causing her unhappiness, all the while knowing the enemy was himself.

He lowered his head to inhale the clean, feminine aroma of her silken curls, and was suddenly aware of the exquisite feel of her breasts crushed to his chest, her slender, soft form molded to his rugged body. She was delicate, fragile, and instead of protecting her as a man should, he was causing her to cry as though her heart were breaking.

"Tessa," he said, not realizing he'd spoken her name aloud. "Tessa."

In her haze of misery, Tessa vaguely heard her name, then it came again, clearer, louder. She slowly registered the fact that she was weeping while being held in Dominic Bonelli's strong arms, and had no idea how she had gotten there.

She stiffened, then attempted to remove her arms unobtrusively from around Dominic, with the irrational hope that he wouldn't have noticed they had ever been there.

She stared straight ahead, appalled by the wet spots on his shirt caused by her tears, along with a smudge of lipstick. As she eased farther away, she realized that he was not releasing her.

"Tessa?"

She snapped her head up to look at him, then inwardly groaned as she remembered how puffy her eyes became when she cried, how blotchy her skin, and how red her nose must be. She was *not* a "pretty crier."

"I'm sorry," Dominic said quietly. "I'm terribly sorry that I upset you like this."

Of all the things that Dominic might have said at that moment, an apology was the last thing that Tessa had expected to hear. She opened her mouth to reply, then closed it, realizing she didn't know what to say.

She should, she told herself, tell him to remove his arms...those strong, nicely muscled arms...from her person. And she would. In a minute.

Her own arms were now hanging uselessly by her sides. Not only was she speechless, but she had no idea what to do with her hands. She felt like a gawky adolescent.

"Your nose is pink," Dominic said, smiling slightly.

"Yes, well..."

His smile faded. "Tessa, listen to me for a minute." He still didn't release her. "I know it wasn't your fault that Joe discovered that Jason is a Bonelli. Okay? You said I tried to dump the paternity of Jason onto one of my brothers."

"*Dump* wasn't a very nice word to use, I guess," she said, now staring at a button on his shirt.

Tessa, she ordered herself, *move away. You're still being held fast by a man you don't even like.* But it felt so good to be encased in strength, to not have to be so incredibly strong on her own, alone. She was so tired and drained. She needed to lean, just for a moment.

That Dominic was the cause of her distress was somehow not important right now. She was going to give herself this time as a gift.

"Tessa, look at me," Dominic said.

When she slowly shifted her gaze from the button to the obsidian depths of his eyes, her breath caught. He was looking at her with tenderness, a gentleness that she'd not seen before. And there, too, was a flicker of...yes, a haunting pain.

She knew with a surprising sureness that Dominic would not want her to see that pain, that a man of control such as he would be angry at himself for revealing any weakness, any hint of vulnerability.

A warmth suffused her that was born of compassion combined with a glowing ember of desire that she wished to deny, but knew she couldn't.

"Yes?" she said, hearing the thread of breathlessness in her voice.

"Tessa," he said, then cleared his throat. "Tessa, I honestly believed that one of my brothers was responsible for fathering Jason. That trip to Las Vegas was many years ago, and my memories of it were dimmed by time. Or so I thought.

"What I now know is that the blur of details was caused by my brothers topping off my drinks so I would really celebrate the event of opening my own firm. They did it *for* me, Frank said, not *to* me, feeling I'd earned the right to have a great time."

"And?" she said, hardly breathing.

"Because of what I learned at the family meeting, I've acknowledged the fact that Jason is...Jason is my son."

"Oh, God, you're not going to demand custody of him, are you? Dominic?" Fresh tears filled her eyes. Without realizing it, Tessa raised her hands to rest flat on Dominic's damp shirt. "You're not going to take my baby, are you? Oh, please, please, no."

Tessa's anguish ripped through Dominic like a burning spear, tearing at him.

He was the cause of her torment.

Only *he* could comfort her.

Two tears slid down Tessa's cheeks.

A moan rumbled in Dominic's chest, then he lowered his head, and kissed her.

And he was lost.

He pulled her close to his body, parted her lips to delve his tongue into the darkness of her mouth and drank of her sweetness. Desire, hot and instanta-neous, coiled low and tight within him.

How long had he been waiting for this kiss? he wondered in a haze of passion. Forever, it seemed, as he filled his senses with the taste, the feel, the tanta-lizingly feminine aroma of Tessa.

Tessa was swept away. She returned Dominic's kiss in a total abandon that was a confused mixture of shock at her behavior, along with a wondrous feeling of rightness.

She was awash with desire, the glowing ember bursting into licking flames. Her breasts were crushed to the hard wall of his muscled chest in a strangely ex-quisite pain. She met his tongue boldly with her own, stroking, dueling, glorying in the existence of his arousal pressing heavily against her.

The kiss went on and on—and it was ecstasy.

Dominic slid his hands over the gentle slope of her buttocks, urging her closer yet. She encircled his neck with her hands, inching her fingertips into the thick depths of his hair.

He raised his head to draw a quick, ragged breath, then sought her lips once more, hungry, urgent, and Tessa answered his ardor in kind.

Time lost meaning. They could only feel, savor, heated desire raging like a brush fire out of control.

Then slowly, Tessa registered a sensation like insid-ous fingers tapping, tapping, demanding attention, accompanied by a whispered message she couldn't decipher. It gained volume, shouting at her louder and louder.

Jason! Jason! Jason!

She tore her mouth from Dominic's and stepped back so quickly, he was forced to release her. She staggered slightly, wrapped her hands around her elbows in a protective gesture, then took a shuddering breath.

"Dear heaven, what am I doing?" she said.

"Tessa," he said, reaching for her. His voice was raspy, husky with passion.

"No," she said, moving farther back. "This is wrong. It should never have happened."

"Oh, no, Tessa, it was right. Very, *very* right."

"No! You didn't answer my question, Dominic," she said, a frantic tone creeping into her voice. "What about Jason? Tell me, damn you, are you going to try to take my son from me? Are you, Dominic?"

He stared at the floor of the porch, seeing the distance now separating him from Tessa. A feeling like nothing he'd ever experienced before washed over him in a chilling wave. He felt empty, hollow, like a shell with nothing within.

He was totally alone and for the first time in his life, he was lonely.

"No," he said, his voice low and flat. "No, Tessa, I won't seek custody of Jason. He's the child of your heart. He's my son by virtue of biology, a fact he's never to know. I'll see to his financial and material needs. I won't take your baby from you. He'll be to me just one more responsibility."

Chapter Twelve

The rush of relief and joy that swept through Tessa caused her knees to tremble. She reached out toward the swing that suddenly appeared terribly far away. She could feel the color draining from her face, and black dots danced before her eyes.

"Hey, whoa," Dominic said as she teetered unsteadily on her feet.

He stepped forward, lifted her into his arms as though she weighed hardly more than a feather pillow, then sat down on the swing with her on his lap. He kept one arm around her just below her breasts, the other across the top of her knees.

Tessa took a deep breath, let it out, shook her head slightly, then blinked.

"I'm all right," she said, not looking at Dominic. "I was just dizzy for a moment. I've been very stressed-out lately, very worried. Well, I'm just fine now, no problem. So! If you'll unhand me, sir, I'll get off of your lap, because there's no reason for me to be here."

"Isn't there?"

Dominic's voice was so low and rumbly, so incredibly *male,* that Tessa shivered. She was acutely aware of the rock-hardness of his thighs and the strength of his arms. The heat emanating from him was weaving through her, and her pale cheeks became flushed.

There were definite reasons that she *shouldn't* be perched on Dominic's lap. He was dangerous, very dangerous. The passion he'd evoked in her was like nothing she had ever known before. He was too powerful, not just physically, but in his ability to throw her totally off kilter.

"Tessa?"

She turned her head slowly to meet his gaze, and saw the smoky hue of desire still evident in his dark eyes. He was so close to her, so close. She had only to lean slightly forward to capture his lips and once again experience the ecstasy of his kiss....

"Kissing you was *not* wrong, Tessa. It was right, for both of us. You gave as much as you received."

"I don't want to talk about it, Dominic."

He looked directly into her eyes for a long moment.

"All right. We won't discuss it further. Now. You can *think* about it, instead."

Oh, thanks, she thought crossly.

She picked up Dominic's arm that was across her knees and moved it away. Shooting him a quick glare, she scooted off his lap to stand in front of the swing. She fiddled with straightening her blouse, then looked at him, lifting her chin.

"I want to thank you," she said, "for relieving my greatest fear that you might seek custody of Jason. There aren't words enough to tell you how much..." Her voice trailed off and she threw up her hands in a gesture of frustration. "See? I hope you know how grateful I am."

"He's your child, Tessa. I wouldn't take him from you." He paused. "I should prepare you for the fact that my family intends to welcome you into the fold. They'll be inviting you and Jason to take part in an event of some sort very soon, I would imagine."

"Oh," she said, her mind racing. She wrapped her hands around her elbows. "What do they plan to say? I mean, how do I explain all this to Jason?"

Dominic shrugged. "That's up to you. They won't tell him who his father is, that much I know. They're determined to make Jason and you members of the clan. They realize you're Jason's aunt, that he doesn't know that, and it won't be divulged. In their minds, you're his mother. You two are to reap the rewards of a large extended family. My wishes on the subject didn't come into play."

Tessa sat down on the swing, angled so she could see Dominic clearly.

"You don't want us there," she said, "with your family?"

Dominic frowned and dragged a restless hand through his hair.

"I wasn't given time to even think about it, was simply *told* how things were going to be. I don't like being dictated to, Tessa, about anything. I haven't spoken to anyone in my family since that meeting Thursday night."

"I see," she said quietly.

He *didn't* want her and Jason interacting with his family, she thought. There was a painful knot in her stomach. That realization hurt her, which was ridiculous. Why should she care if Dominic did, or did not, want her underfoot? It didn't matter one way or another.

But Jason? He didn't even wish to witness his son being a part of the Bonelli family? He now acknowledged that Jason was his child. Didn't that mean anything to him? He had said he'd view Jason as one more responsibility. Dear heaven, how cold and empty that sounded. What about love? Hadn't Dominic even considered that he might come to love his son?

Tessa, stop it, she told herself. She should count her blessings and be eternally grateful that Dominic had no intention of exploring any deeper emotions regarding Jason. A "responsibility" was a nonentity, a "thing" he had to tend to. It was safer in the long run for her and Jason if Dominic stayed emotionally detached.

But how could a man do that with his own son?

A part of her wanted to shout with joy that Jason was hers, the threat of losing him gone. Yet, she was also sad that Dominic refused to interact as a father with Jason, give his child a father's love.

Her mind was becoming a muddled maze once more. As of that moment, she refused to think about *anything*.

"Where's Jason?" Dominic said, bringing Tessa from her tangled thoughts.

"What? Oh." She glanced at the sky, seeing the last streaks of the sunset beginning to fade in the gathering dusk. "He should be home soon. He's in town playing with Jeremiah. Poor little Jeremiah has chicken pox and was so bored. His mother drove out and—"

Dominic lunged to his feet to tower over Tessa. His sudden motion caused the swing to wiggle wildly. She shifted against the back, and looked up at him in shock.

"You allowed Jason to spend time with a child who has chicken pox?" Dominic said none too quietly. "I assume Jason has already had them."

"Well, no, he hasn't but—"

"Then what in the hell is he doing playing with this Jeremiah kid? Good Lord, Tessa, where was your common sense?"

Tessa jumped to her feet and curled her hands into fists planted on her hips.

"You just hold it right there, mister," she said, matching his volume. "Don't you dare question my decisions as Jason's mother. Not ever."

"We're talking about a contagious disease, lady!"

"Oh, shut up, Bonelli. I have enough brains to know that chicken pox are contagious. Jeremiah shared them with everyone at Rainbow's End. Jason has been exposed and I fully expect him to be a polka-dot cowboy in a couple of weeks. The damage is done. There's absolutely no harm in his being near Jeremiah now."

She pointed one finger in the air.

"And another thing. It has been medically proven, Mr. Bonelli, that childhood diseases are best dealt with as a child. If Jason has chicken pox at five, he won't miss school later, *and* he won't run the risk of getting them as an adult and perhaps being seriously ill."

"Oh. Well, how was I supposed to know all that?"

"Why should you care?"

"Damn it, he's my son!"

A sudden heavy silence fell as the impact of Dominic's statement hung in the air. They stared at each other, expressions of confusion on both of their faces.

Dominic finally exhaled a pent-up breath that puffed out his cheeks, then dragged both hands down his face.

"Man," he said quietly, "I'm a mess. My mind is spaghetti." He chuckled, and then shook his head. Tessa sure was on a rip. "You're something, Tessa Russell, you really are," he said, matching her smile. In the next instant, he was serious again. "This whole thing blindsided me. I'll get a handle on it, though. But I don't want you to worry further that I might seek custody of Jason. I won't. I just need some time to adjust to the fact that he's my son.

"I never intended to have a wife and children because I've had the responsibility of a large family since I was fourteen years old. And I'm *still* responsible for them, always will be, I guess. Don't worry, I'll get Jason's existence into perspective."

"Just another Bonelli in a long line of Bonellis," Tessa said, frowning.

"Well, no, not quite. I have an even greater sense of responsibility toward Jason. When I thought he was the son of one of my brothers, I wanted him, as a Bonelli, to live in a house that was sound, in proper repair."

Tessa opened her mouth to retort, but Dominic raised one hand to silence her.

"Don't spin into a tizzy. When you get that temper of yours going, you're a handful, and I'm one exhausted man."

"Mmm," she said with an indignant little sniff.

"Believe me, Tessa, I respect what you've done with your life and the way you've provided for Jason. You're to be commended for starting Rainbow's End from scratch, devising a means whereby you could be with Jason on a daily basis and still earn a living. You've carried a helluva load on your shoulders."

"Oh, well . . ." She shrugged.

"I'm not diminishing anything you've done. If you view this from a practical standpoint, it's very simple. I'm in a position to smooth out the rough edges, such as a leaky roof, faulty plumbing, a coat of paint here and there.

"Jason deserves that, and so do you, as a matter of fact. I can provide those things, and I intend to do it. I'll also set up a trust fund for his college education, and give you monthly support payments."

"No."

"Yes. Jason is not just another Bonelli in a long line of Bonellis. He *is* my son. Therefore, my responsibility for him is greater than it is for my sisters, brothers, nieces and nephews. Does this make sense to you?"

It was all so cold, so clinical, Tessa thought. She was really getting tired of hearing Dominic say the word "responsibility."

"Does it?" he said.

Tessa sighed. "I suppose so."

"Good. Well, I'd better shove off."

Then Tessa glanced up and saw a cloud of dust in the distance, along with the bobbing headlights of a car.

"Dominic, wait. I'm fairly certain that's Jeremiah's mother driving this way. Jason has talked about his friend Dominic coming to visit him. I tried to explain that you're very busy and might not be able to come out here, but he was adamant, convinced you would. It would mean a lot to him if you could stay a few minutes to say hello."

Dominic looked in the direction of the approaching vehicle.

"Sure," he said. "No problem."

Then why, he wondered, was his heart suddenly thudding like a bongo drum? Dumb question. Easy answer. This would be the first time he'd seen Jason since learning that the boy was his son. Well, fine. That was the reason he'd come all the way out here... to see Jason and put him in the proper slot in his mind.

He had *not* driven to Rainbow's End with the intention of kissing Tessa Russell. But kiss her he had, and it was not going to be easily forgotten. He hadn't wanted to *stop* kissing her. The bottom line? He'd wanted to make love with her, had ached with that need.

Crazy. It was really crazy. She wasn't his type. She didn't play the fast-lane game of no commitments, no tomorrows. Tessa was hearth, home and motherhood, the kind of woman he stayed a hundred miles away from.

But, oh, how he'd wanted her.

Understandable, he assured himself. He was emotionally drained and her tears had caught him off guard. Plus, she was an attractive, sensuous, *very sensuous,* woman who had responded completely to his kisses. There was an extremely passionate female within the fresh-air-and-sunshine, jean-clad exterior of Tessa Russell.

Fine. He'd figured out why she'd been capable of ying him in knots, why he'd wanted her with an intensity far beyond anything he could remember expeiencing before. And that was that.

The car stopped in front of the house, Jason got out and hollered "''Bye" as he slammed the door. Jereniah's mother tooted the horn and waved at Tessa before turning the car around and driving away.

Even in the rapidly falling darkness, Dominic could clearly see Jason as he ran up the front walkway.

My son, his mind hammered. *This child is my son.*

"Dominic," Jason yelled. "You came to see me. I knew you would. I told you, Mom. Dominic is here."

Jason barreled up the steps and virtually launched himself at Dominic. Out of pure reflex, Dominic opened his arms to catch the human missile. In the next instant, Jason had his legs wrapped around Dominic's waist and his little arms encircling his neck.

"You came to see me," Jason said, beaming.

"Yeah," Dominic said, unable to keep from smiling. "Yeah, I came." He paused. "Whew. You're quite a load, sport. I've never held a five-year-old cowboy before."

He hadn't? Tessa thought, staring at the pair. What did he do with his nieces and nephews? Pat them on the head as though they were cute puppies?

"My gosh, Jason," Dominic said, "you've sure put some miles on your cowboy suit. It *was* bright red, but 's two shades lighter now. The white fringe is missing in spots, too. Been riding the range a lot?"

"Yep," Jason said.

"No joke," Tessa said, laughing. "It's been worn and washed every day since you gave it to him. I mean , he has *not* worn anything other than that suit."

"No kidding?" Dominic said. "That's great, really great. I'm glad you like it, Jason."

"It's my bestis thing in the whole wide world."

"Fantastic," Dominic said.

Oh, look at them, Tessa thought. Even as dark as it was becoming, she could see the mirror images of father and son. The shape of their heads, the tawny skin, the outline of their features, on and on the list went. And the quirky little matching nitches in their ears were there, she knew, hidden beneath the silky thickness of their black hair.

They were beautiful. Both of them.

"Mom," Jason said, "can Dominic have ice cream with us? Please?"

"Oh, honey, Dominic has to leave. He was waiting to say hello to you, but he really has to go back into town now."

"I've got time for a dish of ice cream," Dominic said.

He did? she thought in surprise. "You do?"

"Yippee!" Jason yelled.

"No," Dominic said. "Correct that. I have time for a dish of *gelato.*"

"What?" Jason said.

"*Gelato* is ice cream," Dominic said. "It's time you learned some Italian, kiddo, and *gelato* is a good place to start."

Chapter Thirteen

"Gelato!"

Jason accented his holler with a jump into the kitchen, landing with a loud thud on both feet.

"Gelato!" Jump. *"Gelato!"* Jump.

"Jason, enough," Tessa yelled.

"I can say *gelato*, Mom," he said, sliding onto his chair at the table.

"No kidding," she said dryly, placing a plate of scrambled eggs and bacon in front of him. "Eat your breakfast. It's a new day, a new week, and you can start it off right by cleaning your plate."

Jason shoveled in a forkful of eggs. Tessa sat down across from him with a mug of coffee and a plate containing two slices of raisin toast.

"Don't you think it was really cool of Dominic to teach me how to say *gelato?*" Jason said.

"*Gelato* is cool," she said, then paused. "That's a joke, Jason. *Gelato* is ice cream, which is cold, as in *cool*. Get it?"

"Oh," he said, nodding. "Yeah. Dominic said he'd see me again soon."

"Yes," she said wearily. "I heard him tell you that last night."

What she'd heard and observed during Dominic's extended stay to have a dish of ice cream—forever to be known as *gelato* apparently—had simply added to her state of confusion.

Dominic, she mused, *was a walking, talking contradiction.* He'd firmly declared that Jason was to be nothing more to him than a financial responsibility.

Then he'd turned right around and joined them for a snack, laughing and talking with Jason as though they were best buddies. And if that wasn't muddling enough, Dominic had decided that it was time Jason learned some Italian, for Pete's sake.

Tessa sighed, then nibbled absently on a corner of toast.

She'd dreamed about Dominic. She'd realized that the moment she'd opened her eyes this morning. The dreams had been vivid and sensual. They'd been kissing, touching, reaching for each other time and again.

The backgrounds had shifted, one into the next. They'd been on the porch, then in a vast field of wild flowers. Her jeans and blouse had suddenly been replaced by a gorgeous full-length, pale blue dress that swirled around her like gossamer wings. She'd been so beautiful, Dominic so handsome in a tuxedo, and they'd been dancing in a huge, crowded ballroom.

He'd kissed her again, a searing, heated, hungry kiss that had consumed her with passion. Then...

"Mom?"

Tessa blinked and stared at Jason for a moment as she came back to earth. "What can I do for you, sir?"

"You look weird, or somethin'. You gots a funny smile on your face."

"I do? I did? Oh, well, I was thinking about something funny. Eat your eggs."

Funny? she mentally repeated. *Not even close. Dangerous was the word that applied.* When Dominic had touched her, kissed her, held her, she'd melted, simply dissolved. The remembrance of it all, even the mere memories, caused desire to thrum within her, low and hot. The man was a masculine menace, and she wasn't getting within ten feet of him again.

"Mom," Jason said, "somebody's at the door."

"Oh." She got to her feet, then looked at Jason. "Eggs, mister."

"Gelato!" Jason said as she left the room.

"Give me strength," Tessa muttered.

At the door, she greeted Joe Bonelli pleasantly, then invited him in.

"How are you?" he said, a serious expression on his face.

"Never better," she said, breezily waving a hand through the air.

"Then why aren't you smiling?"

"I'm *not* smiling?" She plastered a bright smile onto her face. "There."

"Nice try, no cigar. Have you heard from Dom?"

"Oh, my, yes. The man in question was here last evening. He told me about the Bonelli family meeting, how you all shoved Jason and me down his throat, as far as informing him we were to be invited to outings and what have you, and that no one will divulge the truth to Jason.

"Dominic plans to be financially responsible for his son, but not acknowledge him." *And Dominic Bonelli had kissed her senseless.* "That's that."

"Dom was furious at that meeting," Joe said. "Man, was he hot. I was wondering if my best suit needed to go to the cleaners before I was buried in it. You should have seen my mother, Tessa. She stood toe to toe with Dom, and told him the way it was going to be. That was something to behold."

"Really?" Tessa said, a genuine smile now appearing. "Oh, I would have loved to have seen that discussion."

Joe chuckled. "It was something, all right. Frank and I were shaking in our shorts. We're staying clear of Dom until he cools off."

"Hi, Joe," Jason said, running into the room. "Wanna hear me say *gelato?*"

"No," Tessa said.

"Gelato!" Jason boomed.

"I may never eat ice cream again," Tessa said, rolling her eyes heavenward.

"Gelato, huh?" Joe said, smiling at Jason. "Who taught you how to say ice cream in Italian?"

"Dominic. He's my friend. He said I should learn Italian stuff. I couldn't wear my cowboy suit today 'cause it was too late for my mom to wash it. Can you say Italian stuff?"

"Sì," Joe said, nodding. He held out his right hand. *"Diventare amici."*

"What's that? What's that?" Jason said, hopping up and down.

"To make friends," Joe said, "or to be friends. Shake on it, pal."

"Cool," Jason said, pumping Joe's hand. "Italian stuff is so neato. Cool, cool, cool. I'm going to tell all the kids how to say *gelato.*"

"Oh, dandy," Tessa said.

"Hey, Joe," a man called from outside. "Are we doing this, or taking a nap?"

"Get started," Joe hollered over his shoulder. "I'll be right there." He looked at Tessa again. "We're going to start stripping the paint off your house today. We'll be using a heat gun to blister up the old paint to make it easier to scrape off, with less mess. You won't have to worry about the kids because we don't let the debris fly around."

"Yes, all right," Tessa said.

"I'll bring in some charts so you can pick the color you want. Hey, Jason, what color do you want your house painted?"

"Red. Just like my cowboy suit."

"No," Tessa said, laughing. "Oh, good grief, no."

An hour later, Tessa told Joe the number of the little box on the chart that showed the color she'd chosen for the exterior of the house.

An hour after that, she realized she'd picked the same pale blue shade of the beautiful dress she'd worn in her dream about Dominic.

That evening, Tessa had just returned to the living room after reading a story to Jason and tucking him in bed, when the telephone rang. She sat down on the sofa at the same time as she picked up the receiver.

"Hello?"

"Tessa? This is Delores Bonelli."

Oh, my goodness, Tessa thought with a flicker of panic. *Dominic's mother.*

"Hello, Mrs. Bonelli," she said, hoping her voice was steady.

"No, no, call me Delores." She paused. "Tessa, I would have preferred to have this conversation in person, but Joe explained that you're very busy during the day at your Rainbow's End, and your evenings must be spent tending to Jason."

"Yes. Yes, I am busy through the day, and Jason just went to bed."

"So this call will just have to do for now. I'm so eager to meet you and Jason. We're planning a family barbecue here at my home Sunday afternoon at three, and I'm hoping you'll agree to come."

"Well, I don't know, Mrs.... Delores. Dominic isn't pleased in the least with your plans to include me and Jason in your family activities."

"*Your* family, Tessa. Yours and Jason's. I realize that Dominic is being difficult, but I'm ignoring him for the moment. I'll invite him to the barbecue, but I doubt he'll attend. You've met my other sons, so we won't *all* be strangers to you. When you first arrive, you can tell me quietly what you've said to Jason regarding who we are, and I'll let the others know.

"You can be assured that your wishes will be respected. None of us will tell Jason who his father is, either. Will you join us?"

Tessa took a steadying breath before she answered.

"Yes, Jason and I will be delighted to attend. Is it potluck? Shall I bring something?"

"Yes, it *is* potluck. Since you're a member of our family and not a guest, how about bringing a dessert?"

"That will be fine."

"Would you like someone to pick you up?"

"No, I'll drive in if you'll give me directions to your house."

A few minutes later, Tessa replaced the receiver, then pressed her hands to her cheeks.

Dear heaven, had she done the right thing? She could have politely refused Delores's invitation, making it clear that she and Jason were *not* going to be swept up into the Bonelli family.

But she knew deep within her heart that that wouldn't be fair to Jason. There was no reason for him to grow up with only her as his family, when a loving group of people were ready and willing to welcome him into their embrace.

Okay, Tessa, she told herself, *admit it. She* wanted to be part of a large family, too. She'd been so alone for such a long time, and the image in her mind of the Bonelli clan brought an instant smile to her lips.

And Dominic? Oh, heavens, what about Dominic? He was confusing her in so many ways. He said one thing about his responsibility-only relationship with Jason, then turned right around and did just the opposite. Jason was enthralled with his new friend; he thought Dominic was wonderful. He had definitely made an impression on Jason.

"What about you, madam?" she said aloud.

Impression was too lightweight a word for the impact Dominic Bonelli had had on *her*. The man had thrown her totally off kilter and awakened her femininity. He had evoked a desire within her that continued to smolder like a glowing ember.

Well, she was aware of it and, therefore, was in control of it. She'd interact with Dominic just as she did with all the other Bonellis. She'd be chatty, friendly—just another member of the family.

As for the barbecue on Sunday, Delores had said she didn't expect Dominic to even be there. Fine. The first gathering with the Bonellis would be less stressful without Dominic there.

Yes, everything was under control. *Her* control.

The imperative thing to concentrate on now was how to explain to Jason who the Bonellis were. It was so important for her son's emotional well-being that she handle this in the correct manner. She'd use the time available to her between now and Sunday to carefully outline what she would tell him.

And she would not spend one minute dwelling on Dominic Bonelli.

Early Sunday afternoon, Tessa smoothed chocolate icing over the two-layer chocolate cake she'd baked. Jason sat at the table, busily licking a chocolate-coated spatula.

The outside of the house was now painted the lovely shade of pale blue that Tessa had chosen. The crew had returned yesterday to paint the porch and trim white so it would have time to dry before the children returned to Rainbow's End on Monday. She and Jason were using the back door during the weekend.

She finished the cake, placed it carefully in a carrier, tended to the dishes, then sat down opposite Jason at the table.

"Jason," she said, "I'd like to talk to you."

"'Kay," he said, still licking the spatula.

"There's not a speck of chocolate left on there." he reached over and took the spatula from his hands. "You'd best quit licking before I don't have a spatula."

"That was yummy," he said.

"Good. Sweetheart, do you remember the story we read sometimes about the lonely little bunny?"

"Sure. That's Buddy Bunny."

"Why was he lonely?"

"'Cause he didn't have a family like the other bunnies, 'cause he lost them when he was a baby bunny, but he didn't know that, 'cause babies don't 'member stuff good."

"Right. Then he met a bunny who *did* remember Buddy's family, and he took him to meet them."

"And he was happy, happy, happy. Can I have some *gelato*?"

"No, not now. That spatula of icing was your snack. Jason, sometimes *people* have a family they didn't know about."

"Like Buddy?"

"Yes, just like Buddy."

"That would be cool."

"Well, that's exactly what has happened to you, to us. I have you, you have me, but now there are others in our family, too. It's all too confusing to explain to you, but what it means is that you have a grandmother, aunts, uncles and cousins." *And a father, Jason. You have a father but, God help me, I can't tell you that.* "We have a big family, Jason, who are very excited about meeting you."

Jason's eyes widened and he sat up straighter in the chair.

"Really, Mom? Really for honest?"

"Really for honest," she said, nodding. She smiled at him warmly.

"Who are they? Where do they live? Can we go see them?" He jumped off the chair and grabbed her hand. "Come on, Mom, let's go get them."

"We'll go this afternoon. We'll have bubble baths, change our clothes, then it will be time to go."

"Wow. Neato. Who are they?"

"The . . . the Bonellis, Jason." She lifted him onto her lap. "The Bonellis are our family."

"Dominic? Dominic is my family?"

"Honey, listen. We're going to a picnic, a barbecue. Joe, Frank, Vince and Benny will be there, and lots of other Bonellis. Dominic won't be able to come, though."

Jason frowned. "Why not? Doesn't he want to see me find my lost family like Buddy Bunny did?"

"Of course he does, but he's very busy. You like Joe and the others you've already met, and there are more for you to get to know. There will be kids for you to play with, too. Those are your cousins. It's going to be wonderful, you'll see. That's why I baked the cake. We're taking it to the picnic."

"*Buono!*" Jason yelled, sliding off her lap. "That means 'good.' Joe taught me that. Can I wear my cowboy suit?"

"No, not this time. It's worse for wear, you know. I'd like you to look very nice."

"Oh. Well, okay. This is *buono*, Mom. We gots a family. A family, Mommy. Don't you think this is super, really neato?"

"Yes." *I hope so, Jason. Oh, dear Lord, I hope I'm doing the right thing.* "Now, off to the bathtub. You can go first."

Jason started toward the door, then stopped, turning to look at Tessa again.

"Mommy?"

"Yes, honey?"

"Now that we found our family, they won't get lost again, will they? Buddy Bunny got to keep his family when he found them. Can we be with the Bonellis forever, Mom?"

The achy sensation of threatening tears clutched Tessa's throat.

"Forever, Jason," she whispered. "I promise. We won't lose our family now that we've found them. We won't lose them ever again."

Chapter Fourteen

Just after five o'clock, Dominic parked next to the last car in the row of vehicles in front of his mother's house. As he turned off the ignition, he could hear the mingled sounds of children's laughter and the shout of adult voices in the distance, reaching him through the open windows of his car.

He folded his arms over the top of the steering wheel, leaning forward as he stared out the front window.

In his mind's eye, he could clearly envision the scene taking place in the large yard behind the house. He'd attended gatherings such as this countless times in the past, although he'd made only quick, token appearances on numerous occasions.

On the thick carpet of green grass, a volleyball game would be in progress between the adults of the clan interested in taking part in the strenuous sport. Oth ers would be sitting in lawn chairs in the shade of the tall mulberry trees, keeping watch over the children as they played.

A long picnic table that Frank and Benny had built years before would be covered in the traditional red-and-white-checked vinyl cloth. His brothers had constructed the table so that as the family grew in numbers and added space was needed, another section could be easily attached.

There would be high chairs, playpens, a multitude of toys and a group of diaper bags. The half-dozen barbecues would be standing in a row, the coals now beginning to glow, at the ready to receive the towers of thick steaks piled on platters.

Yes, he mused, he knew exactly what was happening beyond his view behind the house. Only this time, there was a major difference.

Tessa was there.

And so was Jason.

His son.

Dominic sighed and sank back in the plush seat.

Why had he come? He'd had no intention of attending this barbecue. That decision had been firmly in place when he'd awakened that morning, but as the hours of the day crept slowly by, his solid resolve had begun to crumble, chipped away by the silence and solitude within the walls of his house.

Images of Tessa had taunted him, and the remembrance of the kisses shared with her had caused heat to coil low and aching in his body.

When he'd forced his thoughts away from Tessa, they fell on Jason. Jason, with his sparkling dark eyes, excited laughter, and the memory of how incredible it had been to hold the little boy in his arms.

Then Tessa would nudge her way back into his mental vision. He'd see her crying, her pain his own. He'd see her smiling. He'd see her lips moist from his kisses, and her expressive brown eyes smoky with desire, with the want of him.

Back and forth, his mind had gone. Back and forth. Tessa. Jason. Tessa. Jason.

Unable to bear the infuriating torment another moment, he'd stormed out of the house in a rage.

And here he was, he thought dryly, hiding in his car like an intimidated kid. Why was he hesitating? Why didn't he just march into the backyard as he normally would?

Was it because he'd taken the stand that the family would not now, nor ever, tell him what to do? Did he feel he'd be losing face, diminish his role as head of the Bonellis by making an appearance at an event *they'd* dictated would take place, without asking for his approval or opinion?

No, damn it, that wasn't it. One Sunday afternoon barbecue couldn't erase the many years of his being in charge, the one responsible for all of them, the one they turned to for advice and guidance.

He was sitting in his car like an idiot because of Tessa, and because of Jason Robert Russell... Bonelli.

"Hell," he said, smacking the steering wheel with the palm of one hand.

He got out of the car, started to slam the door, then closed it with a quiet click followed by a snort of self-disgust.

With heavy steps, he strode along the paved walkway at the side of the house, coming to a halt at the five-foot high, redwood gate. His gaze swept over the yard, seeing everything as he'd imagined it.

He ignored the sudden increased tempo of his heart as he sought, then found, Tessa. She was playing volleyball. There was a bright smile on her face and a vibrant aura of carefree happiness emanating from her as she jumped high to strike the ball.

"Way to go, Tessa," Carmen yelled. "Our point. Our point. We're clobbering you do-nothings."

"It ain't over till it's over, Miss Mouth," Vince called, from the other side of the net.

"One more point and it's over," Tessa said, laughing. "Our serve. Joe, do your stuff."

As the players rotated their positions, Dominic blinked in surprise as he realized he was smiling. He replaced the expression with a frown as he ran one hand over the back of his neck.

Damn, Tessa looked so...so *right* in the midst of his family. She was obviously having fun. She deserved it, and he was sincerely pleased that she was reaping the rewards of being welcomed into the warm embrace of the Bonelli clan.

And Jason? How was he doing? Dominic wondered, his eyes darting around the expanse. Yes, there he was. Lord, he looked so much like the other Bonelli kids, it had been difficult to pinpoint him for a moment.

The older children were playing "wheelbarrow," with Frank's nine-year-old son, Tony, holding up Jason's feet as the boy scrambled on his hands. He was giggling so hard, he lost his balance and toppled forward, rolling around in the grass and laughing.

"Buono!" Jason yelled. "That was *buono*. Let's do it again, Tony."

"We won!" Carmen shouted. "Ho-ho, we beat the socks off you guys!"

Delores suddenly swung a brass bell in the air that was a replica of one used to call students into school in frontier days. Everyone stopped immediately and looked in her direction.

"Attention, attention," she said, beaming. "You all know your assignments. There are little ones needing their hands washed, the food is to be brought out and you boys decide among you who's to barbecue the steaks. We'll need three cooks, per usual. Tessa, you can help bring the food from the house. Jason, *bambino,* go with the others and wash your hands. *Óra di colazione!*"

"Wow," Jason said to Tony. "Nana talks Italian stuff really great. What did she say?"

"It's lunchtime, dinnertime, whatever," Tony said with a shrug. "You know, time to eat. Come on, Jason, I'll race you to the house."

As everyone moved to follow Delores's directives, Dominic stepped back out of view, leaning against the house and closing his eyes.

A chill of loneliness, of total isolation, swept over him with such intensity that he shivered. He opened his eyes and stared up at the heavens.

His family, he thought, didn't need him for anything.

Of course an event as simple as a Sunday barbecue could take place without his supervision. Delores was in her drill-sergeant mode, everyone snapped to attention and loved it. But it went deeper than that. He'd absently realized the other night that it had been a couple of years since a family meeting had been called. That fact hadn't meant anything to him at the time.

But now? The truth hit him like punishing blows. Everyone was set, taken care of, getting on well with their lives. They were making their own decisions. They were *responsible* for themselves.

They didn't need him anymore.

He dragged both hands down his face and drew a shuddering breath.

And Tessa? Jason? Hell, they were obviously doing fine, were comfortable in the midst of the clan and had been accepted as part of the family. Except for sprucing up her house and providing extra money each month, he had no place in Tessa's life, either.

Damn it, Bonelli, he fumed. *What in the blue blazes is the matter with you?* He should be relieved to know that the role he'd had since he was fourteen was at an end. He was free to live his own life, really live it, without looking over his shoulder all the time to determine which family member needed what.

He should feel as though a tremendous weight had been lifted from his shoulders. Yes, he was free to live.

And love?

Dominic stiffened and frowned.

And love? Where had that bizarre thought come from? Love, as in fall in love with a special woman, marry, have children? Join the rank and file of upwardly mobile yuppies with a checklist of hearth, home and two-point-five kids?

Hell, no!

There was no room for that malarkey in his life. He had all he could handle being responsible for the multitude of Bonellis, who looked to him for . . .

Nothing.

"Jason," Tessa yelled, "don't roll around in the grass or you'll have to wash your hands again. Come sit down, sweetheart."

"Can I sit by Tony?"

"You sure can," Frank said. "You two look so much alike, though, I'd better be careful I don't take the wrong boy home."

"I'm bigger than Jason, Dad," Tony said.

Frank laughed. "That you are, son."

"I'm getting bigger," Jason said. "When I grow up I'm going to be tall and have muscles like my friend Dominic."

"Dominic's your friend, huh?" Frank said.

"Yep," Jason said.

Dominic narrowed his eyes. *I'm his father!*

Before he realized he'd moved, Dominic pushed off from the side of the house, opened the gate and entered the yard, slamming the gate closed behind him. The noise caused all heads to turn in his direction, and he stopped dead in his tracks, now acutely aware of what he'd done.

"Dominic!" Jason yelled, running toward him. "You came."

As Jason flung himself at Dominic, he lifted the boy, holding him close.

"Yeah, I came," he said quietly. He didn't know why. He didn't even know if he really wanted to be there but... "I'm here."

"Know what?" Jason said, wrapping his arm around Dominic's neck. "Me and my mom gots family now. We're Bonellis, sort of, 'cause we found our family we didn't know we had 'cause they were lost and... It's like Buddy Bunny. Isn't that neato

You're my friend *and* my family, Dominic. Don't you think that's cool?''

"Very cool," Dominic said, setting Jason back on his feet.

He straightened and swept his gaze over the throng, feeling like a bug under a microscope as everyone continued to stare at him. His eyes collided with Tessa's, and she smiled at him tentatively.

She moved around the table to walk slowly toward him. Her smile grew, the warmth of it reaching the depths of her brown eyes.

"Hello, Dominic," she said, stopping in front of him. "It's nice to see you. Jason and I are having a marvelous time with your wonderful family."

"Say *ciao* 'stead of 'hello,'" Jason told her. "That's Italian. Mom, they're our family, too. That's what you told me."

"Yes," she said, still looking directly into Dominic's eyes. "They're our family, too."

Tessa, Dominic's mind hummed. She was so pretty. She was wearing jeans and a pink string-sweater, her face was flushed with a healthy glow from the exertion of the volleyball game, her hair was a fetching disarray of silky, strawberry-blond curls.

He wanted to kiss her, hold her, feel her feminine softness nestled against him. Heat was coiling low in his body and his heart was beating a rapid tattoo.

Oh, hello, Dominic, ciao, Tessa mused. In jeans and a burgundy-colored knit shirt, he looked tall and massive, so strong, so male. She had the nearly uncontrollable urge to fling herself into his arms and capture his lips with hers to savor the ecstasy of his kiss.

"Who's cooking steaks?" Delores said, breaking the silence in the yard.

Dominic's head snapped up as he tore his gaze from Tessa's.

"I am," he said. "I've never done it before, but how tough can it be?"

"Dom's going to barbecue?" Maria whispered to Carmen, and Frank's wife, Lydia. "Is that weird?"

"I think," Carmen said thoughtfully, "that's Tessa."

"Huh?" Maria said.

"Shh," Carmen said.

"Interesting," Joe said.

"You've got that straight, big brother," Carmen said.

"Huh?" Maria said.

"Shh," Carmen, Joe and Lydia said in unison.

The beehive of activity resumed, along with the volume-on-high chatter. Delores watched Dominic stride across the yard to the row of barbecues, with Jason close on his heels. Dominic hunkered down to speak to Jason, explaining that it wasn't safe for little boys to be near the fires.

"Oh," Jason said. "'Kay. Will you sit by me when we eat? I'm by Tony, and you can be with us."

"What about your mom?" Dominic said.

"She can be by us, too. 'Kay?"

"'Kay," he said, ruffling Jason's hair. "Now scoot, sport."

Jason dashed off and Dominic stepped closer to the barbecues.

"You burn it," Joe said, "you eat it."

Dominic laughed and Delores smiled, looking as if her heart were nearly bursting with love as she gazed at her eldest son.

"*Buono,* my Dom," she whispered. "*Buono.*"

When Dominic sat down next to Tessa to begin the meal, she fully expected to become tense within moments and unable to eat any of the vast selection of delicious food.

To her own amazement, her nerves stayed steady. She was, admittedly, acutely aware of Dominic's proximity, but there was a strange feeling of rightness to his being by her side.

Jason was next to Dominic, then Tony. Carmen sat on Tessa's left. When Dominic reached over to cut Jason's meat into bite-size pieces, Tessa and Carmen exchanged surprised glances, ending with Carmen winking at her.

Everyone managed to eat and talk at the same time. Dominic was kidded good-naturedly about his lack of barbecuing skills, with Frank telling him not to quit his day job, nor to think about becoming a chef.

Tessa had difficulty keeping track of the buzz of topics being discussed, deciding it must take practice to interact with so many people at once.

"Rainbow's End," Carmen said, gaining Tessa's full attention. "I love the name of your day-care center. Do you have a main room where the kids gather?"

"Yes," Tessa said.

"Well, I was thinking it would be fun to paint a big rainbow on one wall. There could be fluffy clouds, and birds, too."

"Oh, that sounds fantastic, Carmen."

"Hold it," Dominic said.

The two women turned to look at him, Tessa surprised he'd heard what Carmen had said as he'd appeared to be listening to Vince.

"You can do the rainbow," Dominic said, "after the interior of the house has been painted. It's going to be done top to bottom. It'll be easier to paint the wall first, than have to go around a rainbow and other stuff. You'll have to wait a week or so, Carmen."

"Paint the interior?" Tessa said.

"That's fine, Dom," Carmen said. "Maybe we'll pick a pale blue for that wall. You know, like a sky, then I can come in and add the clouds, birds and rainbow."

"Paint the interior?" Tessa repeated, but no one paid any attention to her.

"Good plan," Frank said from farther down the table. "We don't want to dink around having to paint the edges of little birds. We'll slap on the sky color *then* you can go nuts, Carmen."

"Yep," Benny said from another direction. "That's the plan. It's a done deal."

"But," Tessa said.

Carmen patted her hand and smiled. "Go with the flow, Tessa. You'll get used to us. You'll come to love us, if we don't drive you crazy first."

Tessa laughed. "Whatever," she said, rolling her eyes heavenward.

You'll come to love us, her mind echoed.

You'll come to love us, Dominic mentally repeated.

They looked at each other at the same time, as though the matching messages in their minds had been heard by the other. Their expressions were questioning, accompanied by slight frowns of confusion. An instant later, they averted their eyes, then feigned in terest in a debate taking place on a movie currently receiving mixed reviews.

The desserts were consumed, then moans and groans followed, with laments of having eaten too much, and the inability to move for a week. Delores announced they could hibernate like well-fed bears *after* the table was cleared.

Darkness was inching its way across the sky, chasing the vibrant sunset to the horizon, as fussing babies were lifted into soothing arms and belongings were gathered.

Lydia approached Tessa, speaking to her in a quiet voice.

"Tessa," she said, "Tony would like Jason to spend the night with us next Saturday. I didn't want to ask in front of Jason. Despite the difference in their ages, they get along great. What do you think?"

"Jason's never spent a night away from home. I can't guarantee he won't change his mind in the middle of the night."

Lydia shrugged. "No problem. I can handle that."

"Well, then I guess it would be fine if he wants to." Tessa paused. "Oh, wait a minute. Jason was exposed to chicken pox about ten days ago. Add another week to that and he's liable to be a speckled cowboy."

"My kids have had chicken pox," Lydia said. "If Jason is still feeling all right, he's welcome to come. If the nasty little spots pop out while he's with us, so be it."

Tessa laughed. "You're a brave soul, Lydia." She Glanced around. "Jason, come here please."

As Jason ran across the yard, Dominic finished helping Benny dump the ashes from the barbecues into a metal pail, then strolled toward Tessa. He heard Tessa explain to Jason the invitation for the following Saturday.

"Wow," Jason said. "Can I go to Tony's, Mom? Can I? Please?"

"If you want to."

"Yes, yes, yes," he said, hopping up and down. "Hey, Tony, guess what?" He took off at a run to find his new friend.

"Hi, Dom," Lydia said, glancing up at him as he joined them. "How do you like barbecuing steaks?"

He chuckled. "My technique needs work."

"Lydia," Frank called, "let's hit the road, babe."

"I'll call you this week, Tessa," Lydia said, "to iron out the details for Jason's sleep-over. It was so wonderful to meet you and your son." She gave Tessa a quick hug.

"Bye for now."

"Goodbye and thank you," Tessa said, then watched Lydia hurry away. "Well, I'd better round up my cowpoke and head for the hills."

"Tessa, wait," Dominic said quietly.

"Yes?"

"Jason is going to be at Lydia and Frank's Saturday night, so that solves your babysitting problem. I was wondering if you'd like to go out to dinner? How does seven o'clock sound?"

Tessa cocked her head slightly to one side, studied Dominic's face and frowned.

"Why?" she said.

"Why?" he repeated, obviously startled by her response.

She folded her arms over her breasts. "Yes. It's a reasonable question. Why do you want to take me to dinner? To discuss additional plans for my house? That would be a novelty. So far, I've been the last to know what's going to be done. Or will you have your briefcase in hand, ready to produce the document I'm supposed to sign? Or—''

"Damn it," Dominic interrupted, none too quietly "I'm inviting you out to dinner because I want to be with you. Is that simple enough for you, Ms. Russell?''

"Sounds plain to me," Carmen said from somewhere in the distance.

"Me, too," Joe added.

"Dinner and dancing," Maria said wistfully. "I remember dancing. That was back when I could see my feet. Pick a place that has a band, Dom.''

"Oh, good Lord," he said, dropping his chin to his chest. "In my next life, I'm going to be an only child, I swear it."

"Tessa," Delores said, "Dominic is getting grumpy. Answer his question."

"Dominic Bonelli," Tessa shouted, then burst into laughter, "I'd be delighted to have dinner with you at seven o'clock on Saturday night!" She dissolved in a fit of giggles.

A cheer went up from the Bonelli clan.

Chapter Fifteen

When the alarm clock rang early the next morning, Tessa shut it off, then stretched lazily while deciding to indulge in an extra five minutes in bed.

She had, she realized, as she became fully awake, a new sense of anticipation about the day. In fact, the entire week held a nice appeal.

It wasn't as though she was accustomed to starting each day in a gloomy mood. During the past five years, she'd considered herself a happy, contented, upbeat person.

But now? Today? Well, there was just so much more in her life than had been there before. The work crew consisting of the warm, fun and friendly Bonellis would be descending again to begin painting the interior of the house. They were part of her and Jason's "sort of" family and were delightful.

Then, later in the week, perhaps, Carmen would come to paint the rainbow, fluffy clouds and the birds on the wall. The children would love it, and she was looking forward to seeing Carmen again.

There was more depth to her existence, a richer, deeper texture made up of wonderful people. Jason, too, was reaping the rewards of having been welcomed into the Bonelli family and she was thrilled for her son.

And to top off the hustle and bustle of the week was her dinner date with Dominic.

"Oh," she said aloud. A frown replaced the smile that had appeared as if of its own volition. "Oh, dear," she added as she remembered.

She'd acted a tad out of character by hollering to the heavens her acceptance of Dominic's invitation. Laughing her head off hadn't been a terrific thing to do, either.

It was just that she'd had such a fantastic time at the barbecue, and Dominic had been a good sport as he'd interacted with his family. He'd actually lightened up. She'd witnessed yet another layer of him and had liked it very, very much.

So, when he'd gotten crabby and slipped back into his ever-so-serious mode, she'd decided not to allow him to dim her happy frame of mind. It was a wonder the man hadn't strangled her on the spot.

Tessa threw back the blankets, left the bed and began to gather clean clothes.

She had a dinner date with Dominic Bonelli on Saturday night, she mentally repeated. How did she *really* feel about that? Dominic had said that he was inviting her out to dinner because he wanted to be with her.

Fancy that, she mused, heading for the bathroom. Well, she wanted to be with *him*, too. The unanswered question that was causing a little curl of fear in the pit of her stomach was whether or not she *should* be going out with Dominic.

She turned on the water in the bathtub, added a scoop of fragrant crystals, then watched the bubbles instantly begin to appear, filling the small room with the delicate aroma of wildflowers. She brushed her teeth, then minutes later sank with a sigh of pleasure into the warm, bubbly water.

Dominic. He was dangerous, no doubt about it. He caused her to lose control of her common sense. When held in his strong arms, she could only feel, savor the ecstasy of his kiss, the awareness of his blatant masculinity.

It was so risky to be near him. She'd vowed to never again relinquish command of her mind, body or heart, and be at the mercy of another's whims.

So, break the dinner date, she told herself.

She sighed as she pulled the stopper free to release the water, and stepped out of the tub, reaching for a towel.

Canceling the date was what she *should* do, but wasn't *going* to do. She *wanted* to go out with Dominic, be the recipient of his charm and undivided attention. She *wanted* to feel pretty and womanly, if even for a few stolen hours. She *wanted* Dominic to kiss her good-night at her door, allow desire to hum through her in a heated current, making her feel alive, vital and feminine.

"Remember that, Ms. Russell," she muttered as she tugged jeans over her bikini panties. "Say goodbye at he door. On the porch. If you invite the man inside when he brings you home, I'll wring your silly neck."

She woke a grumbling Jason, then went downstairs o cook breakfast. As she was whipping pancake bat-er in a bowl, her hand suddenly stilled.

"Oh, good grief," she said to the lumpy batter. "I lon't have a thing to wear Saturday night. Cinderella lid *not* wear jeans to the ball."

Just as she and Jason were finishing breakfast, 'rank knocked on the screen door. He was his usual :heery self, and once Jason's request to have his bed-oom painted red like his cowboy suit was rejected, 'essa chose a soft white for the interior of the house. 'he wall to receive Carmen's mural would be the same hade of blue as the exterior.

The color, Tessa mused, of the beautiful dress she'd vorn in that not-to-be-forgotten dream she'd had .bout Dominic.

Greetings were exchanged with the other Bonellis, hen they tromped up the stairs with a variety of quipment. Joe drove back into town to get more aint, enough being in the truck to get started.

The day progressed in the normal routine, but all he while, Tessa was aware that the Bonelli brothers vere busily at work on the upper level of her home.

She liked that realization, she admitted. She and ason were, indeed, part of a family. The only void in he cozy thought was the lack of Dominic's presence.

Lydia telephoned in midafternoon to confirm Ja-on's visit, providing he wasn't feeling ill due to ap-roaching chicken pox.

"I'll drive Jason into town on Saturday," Tessa aid. "I have some shopping to do." How embarrass-g it would be if Lydia knew Tessa didn't own a dress pretty enough for a dinner date. "What time should I have him at your house?"

"Oh, early afternoon is fine," Lydia said. "I hope you find exactly what you're looking for."

"Pardon me?"

"You're going shopping for a dress for your date with Dominic. Right? Think really sexy, Tessa. Knock him for a loop."

"Oh, well, I..." Her voice trailed off as she felt a flush on her cheeks.

"We're all buzzing about Dominic showing up at the barbecue. Not only that, but the way he acted.. You know, laughing, chatting, paying attention to Jason and the other kids. That's not the Dominic we're used to seeing. You're good for him, Tessa, you really are.

"You, Dominic and Jason look so right together. We're all hoping... Well, as Mama Bonelli says, 'Time holds all the answers.' Delores is a very wise and wonderful woman." Lydia paused. "Now then, let me give you directions to our house for Saturday afternoon. We'll drive Jason home after dinner Sunday evening." She laughed. "Ah, chicken pox. Time holds the answer to them, too."

The following days passed quickly.

Tessa was thoroughly delighted with the fresh, clean appearance of the living area upstairs. Jason declared his room to be *buono*.

The sky-blue wall in the main room downstairs was painted on Wednesday, and Carmen called to say she'd drive out Friday to add the rainbow, clouds and birds.

To Tessa's amazement, the Bonelli brothers managed to work around her as they painted the kitchen

They simply took a break when she needed to prepare snacks or lunches, the men never showing the least bit of irritation or impatience when they had to step out of the way.

The big, old house was full of people, noise, confusion, ongoing activity and seemingly endless laughter. The sound of deep masculine laughter combined with that of Tessa's, Emma's and Patty's, topped off by the gleeful giggles of happy children.

It was as though, Tessa reflected, her home had awakened from a quiet slumber that had been peaceful when only she and Jason were there. But now the house was overflowing with sunshine, was vitally alive during the day, while still offering a safe haven at night. It was perfect.

Carmen arrived bright and early on Friday morning with a smile, a hug for Tessa and Jason and an intriguing array of art supplies.

The children begged to be allowed to watch Carmen paint the rainbow instead of going to the play yard, and Tessa agreed, lining up toy blocks as the barrier they were not to cross while Carmen painted. With awe and wonder on their little faces, the children didn't budge as Carmen worked her magic.

Tessa, Patty and Emma shrugged, sat on the floor behind the children and enjoyed the reprieve from chasing the busy kids.

"Oh, my," Tessa whispered as the rainbow began to take shape. "Isn't that glorious?"

"Carmen is a very talented young lady," Emma said. "She's doing that freehand, just swish and there is. She's a Bonelli, too?"

Tessa nodded.

"They're quite a family," Emma said. "I like them, all of them."

"So do I," Patty said. "They're so... Oh, what word do I want?" She paused. "*Real.* Yes, that's it. They're real, down-to-earth people. As the teenagers say, 'What you see is what you get.'"

Not quite, Tessa thought, frowning slightly. Dominic Bonelli was a lot different. He had many sides to him, layers that were being slowly revealed to her.

Suddenly, Janice's words spoken so many years before slammed against Tessa's mind.

The man has no soul.

A smile formed on Tessa's lips, a gentle smile, a warm, womanly smile.

The man has no soul. No, that wasn't true. Oh, she'd wholeheartedly agreed with the statement at first. When she'd first met him, he'd seemed a cold, hard, controlling man. He'd barked orders and expected them to be carried out to the letter. He'd worn his attorney uniform like a suit of armor and was prepared to battle for victory against anyone who didn't follow his dictates.

But that was then, this was now.

Dominic most definitely had a soul and a heart. He knew how to smile, laugh, demonstrate honest affection and give of himself beyond what his checkbook provided.

He stood, as she did, behind a protective wall. He moved, as she did, tentatively, cautiously from that shield, like a child taking unsteady steps. He'd been robbed, as she had, of childhood and was trying or greater depths of living like a coat never worn before.

Dominic was warm, fun and friendly, just as his brothers were.

Dominic Bonelli was lovable.

Tessa blinked and stiffened, glancing quickly at Emma and Patty to be certain they hadn't somehow read her mind.

Lovable? she mentally repeated. As in, a man a woman could love, fall in love with, be in love with for all time? A man a woman could envision as a husband and the father of her children. *That* kind of lovable?

Yes.

Not that she was the woman in the equation, she quickly told herself. She wasn't remotely interested in marrying. She had no intention of placing her heart and happiness in a man's safekeeping ever again.

Tessa frowned as the image of a faceless woman being held in Dominic's strong arms flitted across her mind's eye.

Oh, dear, she thought, she didn't like that, not one little bit. That was *not* a picture she cared to dwell on, thank you very much.

She had been the recipient of Dominic's exquisite kisses while being held in his gentle but powerful embrace.

She had seen the heated passion in his dark eyes, that spoke of his desire for *her.*

She was the one who had a dinner date with the man in question on Saturday night, by gum, not some nameless bimbo from the high-society, monied arena Dominic no doubt traveled in.

So there!

Tessa Russell, she admonished herself, *stop it.* Shame on you. She sounded about as mature as Jason when he was throwing a tantrum. She was also

making mental noises like a jealous, possessiv
woman, who considered Dominic exclusively hers.

Absurd. Ridiculous. It was a toss-up betwee
whether she should be sent to her room, or carted of
to the funny farm.

But, oh, mercy, the mere thought of Domini
caused desire to thrum within her—hot, so hot. Th
memory of his kiss, touch, aroma, the sound of hi
rich laughter, caused a tantalizing shiver to cours
through her.

And if she went an imaginary step further, inche
toward the fantasy of making love with Domini
Bonelli, her heart, her mind, her very soul, seemed
nearly burst with the realization that it would be wor
derful, beautiful, glorious...

And so very, *very* right.

No, no, Tessa, please, no, she silently begged. Sh
mustn't do this to herself. She mustn't succumb
Dominic's magnetism. She had to run like the dev
back behind her protective wall and remain there, sa
from harm's way and the risk of being shattered int
a million pieces.

"Ladies and gentlemen," Carmen said. Tess
jerked in surprise as she was jarred from her thought
"I hereby present you with your very own rainbo
complete with fluffy clouds and pretty birds."

The children applauded, then jumped to their fee
Tessa, Emma and Patty moved quickly to the front
the room to be certain none of the excited childre
crossed the toy-block line.

"Children, the paint is wet," Tessa said. "You c
have a closer look later." She turned to the artis
"Oh, Carmen, it's fantastic, absolutely incredible."

Emma clapped her hands. "Okay, little guys, let's wash up for lunch. What do you say to Carmen?"

A chorus of "Thank you, Carmen" went up from the pint-size throng, with Jason's *gràzie* thrown in for Italian good measure. The children lined up and marched away with Patty and Emma as Carmen began to pack her equipment. Tessa stared transfixed at the wall.

"Thank you so much, Carmen," she said. "This is such a special gift. I hardly know what to say."

"It was fun. All my critics should be as easily pleased as your gang." Carmen laughed. "If you decide to sell this place, I'll have a Bonelli brother cover my handiwork. I don't think many people would go for a rainbow in their living room."

"I'm not selling this house. It's my home. I'll be here until I'm old and creaky."

"Oh, you never know, Tessa. Life is just full of surprises."

"Well, I can't argue with that. The past weeks have turned my world upside down. I've definitely had a major dose of surprises lately."

"Yep. All set for your dinner date with Dominic tomorrow night?"

"Oh, sure," she said, breezily waving one hand in the air. "It's just a simple let's-go-out-to-dinner thing, you know."

"Right," Carmen said, laughing. "Whatever you say."

"It is!"

"You bet," Carmen said, her smile firmly in place. "I have a date tomorrow night myself, but mine is with a starving artist I somehow got conned into cooking for. Have a quiet moment of sympathetic thoughts for me while you're doing the town with my cost-is-no-obstacle brother.''

"Dinner is dinner," Tessa said, shrugging.

"Mmm," Carmen said, stifling another burst of laughter. She snapped closed a metal box containing jars of paint. "Tessa, I want to show you something on the wall," she went on, her tone and expression now serious. "Come here."

Tessa stepped closer, obviously confused, then looked at the mural where Carmen was pointing. At the base of the rainbow was a tiny, shiny black, old-fashioned pot with handles painted on each side.

"This is your home and your business," Carmen said quietly, "and you named it Rainbow's End. The tradition is to find a pot of gold at the end of the rainbow. But this one is yours, all of it. Only *you* know what you want, what your hopes and dreams are. That's why I left the pot empty. It's yours to fill, not mine."

"Oh, my," Tessa said. "What a lovely thing to do, to say."

"Think carefully, Tessa, about what you'll put in that little pot, about what you truly want to find at the end of your rainbow."

As Carmen left the house, Tessa wrapped her hands around her elbows and stared at the empty pot at the base of the rainbow.

A gasp escaped from her lips as a swirling, blurry shape suddenly seemed to hover above the opening of the pot, then settled with crystal clarity into place.

"Dear heaven," she said, taking a step backward.

Her eyes widened as she stood statue-still, her heart racing. Dominic Bonelli was her pot of gold.

Chapter Sixteen

As Dominic drove toward Rainbow's End on Saturday evening, he told himself he'd left home with plenty of time to spare to allow for potentially heavy traffic.

A moment later, he mentally threw up his hands in defeat and admitted he was ahead of schedule because he'd been restless and edgy, had been staring at a clock in his living room that seemed to stubbornly refuse to move forward.

Lord, he thought, he was like a kid who was nervous about picking up his date for the senior prom. Well, since he hadn't had the money while in high school to attend any proms, maybe he was going through a second childhood. Oh, hell, whatever.

It had been a strange week that had seemed more like a month, he mused. He'd been extremely busy at the office, which wasn't unusual; it had been the events taking place around the perimeter of his existence that were out of the ordinary.

He had, for the first time he could remember, relived the events of a family barbecue. In the past, the gatherings were forgotten by the time he reached home, his mind focused on what awaited him on his desk the next day.

But not this time.

One of the conclusions he'd come to about the barbecue was that he'd had a good time, had actually enjoyed himself. He was a lousy cook, that was for sure, but he'd get the hang of it in the future.

Another fact he'd realized to be true was that Tessa had been right about his brothers. They *were* warm and friendly. They were nice guys.

Their wives were pleasant, Maria's husband was obviously devoted to her and the zillion kids were as cute as a button—buttons who all looked alike. They'd accepted Jason with no question, just as the adults had welcomed Tessa.

Tessa. Jason. Tessa. Jason.

There his mind went again, doing its Ping-Pong ball routine. Back and forth. Back and forth.

Tessa Russell was driving him nuts.

Tessa Russell had taken up residence in his brain and refused to budge.

Tessa Russell was a nuisance.

And he was looking forward so much to the hours ahead that he would spend with her, it was ridiculous.

"Bonelli," he said aloud, "your mind is mud."

He'd invited his mother out to lunch on Wednesday and officially apologized for his less-than-polite behavior at the family meeting. He'd also, striving for a casual tone of voice he hadn't quite pulled off, told her the barbecue had been rather fun. When Delores had raised her eyebrows at his comment, he'd rolled his eyes heavenward.

"Okay, okay, Mother, I had a good time, really enjoyed myself."

"Buono," she said. "I know you did. I was waiting to see if you'd admit it. Tessa and Jason seemed to enjoy themselves, too. They're wonderful, both of them." She paused. "So! You're taking Tessa out to dinner Saturday night."

Dominic chuckled. "That's no secret. She yelled it so loudly, she might as well have announced it on the ten o'clock news."

"Well, you weren't exactly quiet about the fact, either, Dom."

"I know. She gets to me sometimes, and I lose it. Did you notice that her emotions are telegraphed on her face, in her eyes? She couldn't hide what she's feeling if she tried, which she probably wouldn't do because she's open and honest."

"Mmm," Delores said, nodding.

"She's not my type, of course, but she's lovely, quite beautiful in a wholesome, fresh-air-and-sunshine sort of way. She's a great mother. Jason is a lucky little kid."

"Yes."

"Tessa has done a helluva fine job with her life, especially considering she's all alone. I really respect that. Did you hear her laugh? It's infectious, makes a person smile whether they intended to or not. Her laughter reminds me of wind chimes and—" He stopped speaking and frowned. "Who put the nickel in me? I'm blithering on like an idiot."

Delores covered one of his hands with hers on the top of the table and smiled at him gently.

"No, Dom, you're not blithering on. You're changing, and it's long overdue. It's time for you to live *your* life, instead of concentrating on the needs of your family. We're all fine, doing well.

"I can't give you back the years we took from you, but my heart will sing with joy if you really start living for yourself now."

"Right," he said gruffly, pulling his hand free. "I've already figured out that I'm not needed in my role as the head of the family anymore. You don't have to beat me over the head with that fact."

"Oh, Dominic, don't get angry. We're all so very grateful for what you've done for us. But, my *bambino,* it's your turn to have what *you* want as your first priority. The important thing now is for you to get in touch with yourself and discover what you really do want. Think about it, please, Dom. What do you want?"

Dominic turned off the main road and slowed his speed as he headed out of town toward Rainbow's End.

What do you want?

His mother's words had haunted him since that luncheon with her. When he'd managed to push Tessa and Jason from his thoughts, there would be Delores Bonelli tapping him on the shoulder.

What do you want?

The maddening part was, before he could concentrate on the nagging question, Tessa would be there, front-row center in his mind's eye, cluttering up his thought processes.

Damn that woman. What was it about her that made it so hard for him to shake loose of her image, of the remembrance of the kisses he'd shared with her, of how sensational she'd felt in his arms?

Hell, he didn't know.

He just didn't know.

This dinner date tonight, he decided, was a good idea. He'd blurted out the invitation on impulse and hadn't been quite certain afterward if he was pleased with himself or not.

But now, as of this moment, the evening ahead had a definite purpose. Without Jason around, he could view Tessa strictly as a woman with no connection to his son. He'd realize in spades that she wasn't his type, and that would be that.

"Excellent," he said, pressing harder on the gas pedal. "By the end of this date, everything will be under control again. *My* control."

Dominic glanced at the sky.

The days were getting shorter, he realized. Autumn was in full swing. *Changes.* That seemed to be the operative word lately regarding his life. There were just so damn many changes.

Tessa stood in her bedroom with her back to the full-length mirror hanging on the inside of her closet door. She pressed both hands on her stomach, willing the swarm of butterflies to still.

She'd tried the dress on in the store but had been in a cubbyhole-size room in her bare feet. This was truth time.

Light makeup had been applied, a half-slip, panty hose and evening sandals put on, her hair was washed and the curls brushed until they shone. The delicate scent of wildflower cologne had been sprayed on her throat and wrists.

Then she'd floated the dress over her head...and frozen, unable to gather the courage to turn around and look at herself in the mirror.

Oh, this dress, she thought, glancing down. She'd found it in the third store she'd entered, as though it had been waiting for her, calling her name.

It was blue. It was the exact shade of the dress she'd worn in the dream about Dominic, the same color as the outside of the house and the sky on the wall where Carmen had created her magical mural. Beautiful, beautiful blue.

She took a deep breath, let it out, then turned slowly to face the mirror.

"Oh," she whispered. "Oh, my."

She was beautiful.

The dress fell to midcalf in soft folds of chiffon and had a camisole top with tiny straps.

She stepped closer to the mirror and narrowed her eyes as she peered at herself.

Had the top been cut that low when she'd modeled it in the store? Had the narrow white-lace inserts in the bodice been that transparent? Had she been so...so bare?

Of course, dolt, she scolded herself. The creation hadn't been altered by cute little mice as had been done for Cinderella.

She turned one way, then the other, delighting in the feel and look of the skirt as it swung gently, then fell back into place. She made no attempt to curb the smile that formed on her lips as she indulged in continuing to gaze at her own reflection.

She'd never owned such a lovely dress, had never felt so... well, so beautiful. There was just no other word for it. Every inch of her was a declaration of her womanliness, her femininity.

No wonder Cinderella hadn't wanted to leave the ball, she reflected. Grubby Cindy had been transformed into a glorious woman for her stolen night on the town.

With her Prince Charming.

"Oh." Tessa blinked and pulled herself back to reality from the dreamy place she'd drifted to.

Cindy had Prince Charming, she thought. Tessa was going out with Dominic. So, fine, no problem. She'd covered all that in her mind. She was going to have a marvelous evening in the company of an extremely handsome man. The important thing to remember was the plan to bid him adieu on the front porch. *Outside, Tessa.*

"Got that?" she asked her reflection.

With a decisive nod, she picked up a small clutch purse and a white shawl, then left the room, turning off the light as she went.

She was ready.

She was woman.

She was beautiful!

Tessa Russell, Dominic thought, as he entered the house, was exquisite. *Tessa was beautiful.*

"You look sensational, Tessa," he said, not pleased with the raspy quality of his voice. "Very lovely. Very beautiful."

"Thank you," she said, smiling. "You're rather smashing yourself."

Gorgeous, she decided. The man was simply gorgeous. Charcoal gray suit tailored to perfection, crisp white shirt, paisley tie in shades of gray and burgundy, and a silk burgundy handkerchief visible in the top pocket of the jacket. It all added up to gorgeous, accentuating his physique, the tawny hue of his skin, the night darkness of his hair and eyes.

Was she going to survive this man? Maybe not, but what a fantastic way to dissolve into a puddle and die.

Tessa, she ordered herself, *get a grip.*

"Shall we go?" she said. Darn it, she'd been trying for a cool, sophisticated "Shall we go." What she'd actually produced was a squeaky-sounding "Shall we go" that could have been uttered by one of Cinderella's cute mice. "Well, Dominic?"

As if of their own volition, Dominic's hands raised to frame Tessa's face. His heart was beating so rapidly, he could hear the thudding echo roaring in his ears.

He wanted, he *needed,* he thought hazily, to kiss Tessa now, *right now.* It seemed like an eternity since he'd tasted the nectar of her mouth, felt her feminine curves pressed to his body, inhaled her aroma of wildflowers.

She was a vision of loveliness in that pale blue dress. She looked sexy and sensuous and just gazing at her had the blood pounding wildly through his veins.

Dominic lowered his head and his mouth melted over Tessa's, his tongue parting her lips to delve within, savoring the sweetness.

Yes, his mind hammered.

He dropped his hands to encircle her with his arms, nestling her to his heated body. His arousal was instantaneous, heavy and aching.

Tessa's purse and shawl fell unnoticed to the floor as her arms floated upward to entwine Dominic's neck. She returned his searing kiss in total abandon.

Oh, yes, her mind hummed.

Desire thrummed within her, swirling in a hot current that pulsed low and deep. Her senses were heightened as never before, making her acutely and wondrously aware of her own femininity and Dominic's rugged masculinity.

The kiss was ecstasy, she thought dreamily. Dominic tasted so good, smelled so good, like soap and musky after-shave.

Slowly, reluctantly, Dominic raised his head to meet Tessa's smoky gaze.

"You cast spells over me, Tessa," he said, his voice husky with passion. "I don't behave true to form when I'm with you."

"Nor do I when I'm with you, Dominic. It's all so strange and . . . and rather frightening."

His hold on her tightened slightly and he frowned. "Are you afraid of me? Lord, Tessa, I never meant to frighten you in any way."

"No, no, I'm not *physically* afraid of you. If I asked you to drop your arms right now and let me go, I know you would."

"Guaranteed."

"What frightens me is that I don't seem capable of thinking straight when I'm with you. There are new emotions involved that I don't understand." She paused. "Dominic, I was hurt very badly in a relationship years ago, and I have no intention of ever allowing that to happen to me again.

"A part of me says I should put as much distance between us as possible, and yet..." She shook her head. "I don't know. It's all so confusing."

"You've got that straight," he said, managing a small smile. "Look, we're all right. I don't want a serious relationship, either. I've waited too long to be free of so many responsibilities. I've faced the fact that my family doesn't need me as they once did. My life is finally my own to live as I please.

"We're very attracted to each other, Tessa, and we set off sexual sparks when we're together. As long as we keep a clear understanding in our minds of what we *don't* want, we can go as far as we mutually agree upon with what we *do* want. Agree?"

"I...I guess so," she said quietly. "No strings, no commitments, no tomorrows, just the now of the moment we're in."

"Exactly. So, are you ready to go to dinner?"

"Yes."

He released her, then picked up the purse and shawl and handed them to her. As she was about to walk out the door, she turned to glance at the far wall and the empty pot at the end of the rainbow.

As they drove into town, Dominic tuned the radio to an easy-listening station, and soothing music drifted through the car.

Everything was going according to plan, Dominic thought. He was in control, the situation with Tessa was now clearly defined, the boundaries firmly in place. Fine. Great.

Then why in the hell did he feel as though a dark, gloomy cloud was hovering over him?

Tessa looked out the side window, appalled by the realization that tears were prickling at the back of her eyes.

What on earth was the matter with her? she wondered frantically. She and Dominic had *communicated,* just as magazine articles said two people should. They were on the same wavelength regarding the fact that they did *not* want any kind of serious involvement. They could enjoy each other's company. No one would get hurt.

Then why did she feel as though she were about to burst into tears and weep for a week?

Chapter Seventeen

She now *thoroughly* understood, Tessa thought, why Cinderella had wanted to stay at the ball.

The restaurant Dominic had chosen was one of Tucson's finest. The moment they entered the plush establishment, Tessa's strange and confusing gloomy mood dissipated into thin air.

They were led to a small, cloth-covered table. A candle in the center in a hurricane lamp cast a rosy glow. Even though the restaurant was crowded, the seating arrangement had been skillfully planned to afford diners a sense of privacy.

The waiters, to Tessa's wide-eyed amazement, were dressed in tuxedos, and the menus they were handed were oversize, with a flocked front and back and parchment paper inside.

It was the fanciest, most incredible place she'd ever been in, Tessa thought, looking around to savor every detail. Just being here made a person feel special and . . . beautiful.

"Oh, Dominic," she said, leaning slightly toward him, "this is wonderful. It's like something out of a movie, a make-believe setting."

Dominic smiled, instantly realizing it was a genuine smile and that the dark cloud was no longer hovering over him.

Tessa was enchanting, he thought. Her eyes were sparkling with excitement, and there was an endearing childlike quality to her at the moment as she drank in the atmosphere.

He'd eaten here on many occasions in the past, but this was the first time he'd really *seen* it. Tessa's awe and wonder was delightfully infectious.

There were so many things he took for granted: dining in restaurants such as this one, attending concerts and plays, being invited to private, invitation-only showings at art galleries. Seeing those things and more through Tessa's eyes, fresh, new, as though for the very first time, held great appeal.

She *deserved* the finest and he was in the position to provide it for her. She'd made do with too little for too long. Well, that was going to change as of this very night. Tessa was *his* now.

Dominic stiffened and frowned.

Tessa was his now?

Where in the hell had that bizarre thought come from? She wasn't *his*. They'd just discussed the rules of their seeing each other. There would be no commitments, certainly no possessiveness, no nonsense of "I am yours, you are mine."

Tessa was his now.

Bonelli, he told himself, *knock it off.*

They ordered, and their tuxedo-clad waiter had, to Tessa's total delight, a very British accent. Dominic selected, tasted, then approved a fine wine. Salads were placed in front of them on wafer-thin china plates edged in gold trim.

"Thank you for bringing me here, Dominic," Tessa said, smiling. "If I was attempting to be ultrasophisticated, I'd try to pretend I was accustomed to places like this. But that would be silly, because it isn't remotely close to being true. This is glorious and I'll never forget it." She laughed. "Cinderella and I really have a great deal in common."

"Only to a point," he said, matching her smile. "Your evening doesn't have to end at midnight. My car, your coach, isn't going to turn into a pumpkin. I hope. I'd never able to explain *that* to my insurance agent."

Tessa laughed in delight and the wind-chime sound caused a shaft of heat to rocket through Dominic. As she began to eat the salad, he continued to gaze at her, his own plate forgotten.

She was lovely in the glow of candlelight, he thought. Her skin looked like a soft peach, and her hair shone like silken threads. That dress was seductive, alluring, hinting at the feminine bounty beneath.

Tessa was his now.

With a shake of his head in self-disgust, he picked up his fork and began to eat.

Conversation between them flowed easily through the delicious meal. They discussed movies, books, the political scene in Tucson.

Dominic related some humorous tales of Bonelli antics when his brothers and sisters were young.

Tessa then shared some endearing stories from Jason's toddler years.

"You have some wonderful memories of events shared with Jason, don't you?" Dominic said quietly.

"Yes. Yes, I do." She paused and looked directly into Dominic's dark eyes. "He's only five years old, Dominic. There are years of memories yet to come before he's ready to leave home. You created a memory with him the evening you gave him the cowboy suit. It's yours, that memory. Are you going to keep it?"

He frowned slightly. "That's an unusual way to put it, but..." He nodded. "Yes, I'm going to keep it."

"Good. I'm glad."

They smiled at each other warmly, then their smiles disappeared as they were held immobile, unable to move, or hardly breathe. The muted sounds of voices and clinking dishes faded into oblivion, as did the room itself.

They were aware, acutely aware, only of each other. Messages of desire were sent and received with no words spoken. Heat thrummed within them and the sensuality weaving around and through them was nearly palpable.

"Coffee?"

The sudden sound of the waiter's voice caused both Tessa and Dominic to jerk in surprise.

"Oh," Dominic said, "yes, that would be fine. Tessa, would you care for some dessert?"

"No, just coffee," she said, then drew a steadying breath. "Thank you."

Their cups were filled from a sterling silver pot, then the waiter moved on.

Tessa busied herself adding cream and sugar to the steaming liquid, then devoted her entire attention to the process of stirring. She willed her racing heart to resume a normal rhythm, and hoped to the heavens that the raw desire she'd seen in Dominic's eyes hadn't been visible to him in her own.

"Tessa," Dominic said quietly.

"Hmm?" she said, still concentrating on stirring the coffee.

"You said at your house that you were badly hurt in a relationship years ago."

Tessa's head snapped up and she looked at Dominic, a frown on her face.

"Where did that come from?" she said.

"Well, it occurs to me that by protecting yourself against *all* men because of what *one* did isn't fair, not to men *or* you. Something special, rare, could pass you by because you're too wary to run the risk of loving again. You're young, beautiful and you have a lot to offer. Don't you want to spend your life with someone? Rather than being alone?"

Tessa leaned forward, nearly bumping the coffee cup.

"Dominic," she said, "do you honestly believe that is any of your business?"

Yes! his mind yelled.

Tessa was his now.

No! Damn it, what was he doing? Her attitude suited him perfectly, and there he sat doing a hard sell on putting the past behind her and being open, receptive, to love in the present. Was he nuts? Yes, that was it. He'd slipped over the edge into insanity.

"Dominic?"

"I... That is, being a single parent is very difficult. If your mind wasn't so closed against men, Jason might very well have a father."

Tessa straightened and narrowed her eyes. "He *has* a father." She pushed back her chair. "Excuse me. I'm going to the powder room." Shooting him a dark glare, she got to her feet, then hurried away.

Dominic slouched back in his chair and watched her go.

Tessa was mad as hell, he thought, and he didn't blame her. He'd made it sound as though he'd be delighted if she'd get off the stick and find a man to raise his son.

That was *not* remotely close to what he wanted. The idea of Jason calling another man *Daddy* caused a knot to tighten in his gut.

That same faceless man would be Tessa's husband, would kiss, hold, caress her, reach for her in the night and... The hell he would!

Tessa was his now.

Oh, man, he thought, running one hand over the back of his neck. His mind was a maze of confusion. If he didn't know better, he might begin to believe that he was falling in love with Tessa Russell. That was absurd.

He glanced up and saw Tessa crossing the room to return to the table, seeing several men give her appreciative scrutiny.

So lovely, he mused, his gaze riveted on her. The skirt of her dress swung provocatively, accentuating her nicely shaped legs and the gentle slope of her hips. She held herself straight and tall, emphasizing her elegance and grace.

He knew her to be fun and funny, warm, intelligent, a devoted mother, a savvy businesswoman, and she had a temper that could go off like a bomb when she was provoked.

She was everything, and more, that any man would hope to discover in his life's partner.

Was he falling in love with Tessa?

Maybe, just maybe he was. But even if that proved to be true, he wouldn't pursue it. He wanted no part of the multitude of responsibilities that being a husband and father on a daily basis entailed. He'd tend to Jason's material needs from the edge of the boy's existence.

And Tessa?

If his heart overruled the orders from his brain and he *did* fall in love with her, he'd exit stage left from her life immediately.

Bonelli, he thought, with a decisive nod, *you're back under control.*

He got to his feet when Tessa reached the table.

"Would you like to go into the ballroom and dance?" he said. "They have an excellent combo here."

Tessa opened her mouth to decline, having decided during her exodus to ask to go home. She'd been an gered and strangely hurt by Dominic's urgings to find herself a husband, and provide Jason with a father at the same time.

"I . . ." Her voice trailed off.

"Forget what I said just before you left the table, Tessa. I didn't mean it like it sounded. Rather than sit here and dissect it for the next hour, let's just erase what I said and enjoy the rest of the evening." He extended one hand to her. "May I have this dance, Cinderella?" He smiled.

The man, Tessa thought, placing her hand in his, did *not* play fair.

The large ballroom was lighted by a dozen crystal chandeliers that had been dimmed to a soft glow. Small tables with chairs edged the gleaming dance floor, and a combo was playing a dreamy waltz when Tessa and Dominic entered. She placed her purse and shawl on one of the tables, then they moved onto the fairly crowded floor.

Dominic drew Tessa into his arms and began to dance with smooth expertise.

Cinderella, Tessa's mind whispered as the lingering shadows of her anger and hurt fled. *Oh, yes, she was Cinderella at the ball.* Being held in Dominic's arms, swaying to the dreamy music, was heavenly. This was *her* night, and she was going to allow nothing to mar its splendor. She was beautiful, Dominic was beautiful, *everything* was beautiful.

She sighed with pleasure and nestled closer to Dominic.

Dominic nearly groaned aloud as Tessa pressed against him. Coming into the ballroom to dance, he'd decided, would defuse her anger. What he hadn't taken into consideration was the torture it would be to have Tessa in his arms, close, so close, to his heated, aroused body.

He inhaled her aroma of wildflowers, shutting his eyes for a moment to fully savor the delicate, feminine scent. Her breasts were crushed with exquisite softness to his chest, and he could feel the sensuous curve of her lower back where his hand rested.

He was going up in flames.

The song ended and another began. Dominic cleared his throat and eased Tessa away from him just enough to cause her to tilt her head to look at him questioningly.

"Great band," he said, instantly deciding that had been a lame thing to say.

"Yes. You're an excellent dancer, very easy to follow." She smiled. "That's a good thing, because I'm very rusty when it comes to dancing."

"You do very well, Tessa. You sort of…float." He shook his head. "This is a dumb conversation. We sound like strangers struggling to find something to talk about."

"Well…"

"We are *not* strangers. In fact, I feel as though I've known you for a very long time."

"Oh?" she said, laughing softly. "Are you bored yet?"

"Ms. Russell, there is no way on earth that a man could ever be bored around you. There are so many layers, facets to you, that really keep a guy on his toes."

"You're not exactly uncomplicated yourself, Mr. Bonelli."

"So you're not bored, either?"

"Not even close."

They smiled at each other, then Dominic pulled her to him again. They danced on and on, lost in the magic of the Cinderella night.

Much later, the last song was played, and with Tessa tucked next to him, Dominic led her from the restaurant to the car. By unspoken agreement, she snuggled close to him as they drove toward Rainbow's End.

The sensual spell that had been weaving around and through them during the hours of the evening seemed to fill the car to overflowing.

Once out of the surging traffic, Dominic slowed his speed, wishing to delay the end of the time spent with Tessa. They didn't speak, yet the silence was welcome, leaving them free to savor the crackling awareness of each other.

As her house came into view, the light she'd left on downstairs glowed like a beacon in the darkness, and a niggling little voice began to sound in Tessa's hazy mind. It whispered to her, nudging her to remember her earlier vow to bid Dominic good-night on the porch.

Her heart did a funny flip-flop as he maneuvered the car onto the road that would bring them in just minutes to the house.

Well, Cinderella, she thought. *It's pumpkin time.* The glorious hours were over, the last song had been played. She'd step inside that big old house alone, climb the stairs alone, get ready for bed and sleep—alone.

Suddenly, the image of the rainbow Carmen had painted flitted before Tessa's eyes. She saw the empty pot, and remembered Carmen's dictate that it was up to Tessa to fill it with *her* hopes and dreams.

Dominic.

Oh, dear heaven, was she falling in love with Dominic Bonelli?

The thought of his turning from the porch and walking away caused a cold fist to grip her heart. On this night, *her* night, the house loomed too big, empty, too lonely, without Dominic's magnificent presence within its walls.

She wanted him with her, holding, kissing, caressing her, bringing her vitally alive and glorying in her womanliness.

She wanted to make love with Dominic.

But was she falling *in* love with him?

She didn't know. She just didn't know.

Dominic stopped the car, turned off the ignition and opened the door. After getting out, he leaned down to extend his hand to Tessa, indicating she should slide beneath the steering wheel to leave the vehicle on his side.

The instant she stood, he dropped her hand, wrapped his arms around her and kissed her deeply. She parted her lips to receive his questing tongue as she encircled his neck with her hands.

The kiss was urgent, hungry, evidence of the mutual passion that had built within them during the hours they'd danced. Dominic lifted his head, then slanted his mouth the other way, drinking in her sweetness, savoring the taste. His arousal was heavy ot, the ache for Tessa, the need and want of her, overpowering rational thought.

He tore his mouth from hers.

"Tessa," he said, his voice raspy, "I want to make ove with you. You can feel what you're doing to me, know you can. I think...I think I'd better see you o the door. Now."

He brushed his lips over hers, then released her. Reaching back into the car, he produced her purse and hawl, then closed the door. With one of his arms cross her shoulders, they started up the walkway to he porch.

This was it, Tessa thought. In a couple of seconds, he had to make a decision that would have a tremenlous impact on her life.

Her hands were trembling slightly as she took the ouse key from her purse. They crossed the porch to top by the door.

In her mental vision, she once again saw the pot at he base of the rainbow; the empty pot that only she, 'essa, could fill.

Oh, Tessa, she thought frantically, *think.* Whatver decision she made tonight, she would have to quare off against at dawn's light tomorrow. *Think.*

"Your key, Cinderella?" Dominic said, holding out is hand.

Cinderella, her mind hummed. *Yes.* This was *her* ight, her glorious night to fill the rainbow's pot with *er* hopes and dreams. She'd face tomorrow when it ame. *Tonight was hers.*

"Dominic," she said, her voice hushed, "would you ke to come in?"

"Ahh, Tessa," he said, drawing one thumb over her lips, "if I come in, I won't be leaving tonight. If I walk through that door, we'll make love."

She looked at the door, seeing in her mind's eye the pot and the rainbow. The pot suddenly began to glow with a golden light.

"Rainbow's end," she whispered.

"Tessa? Do you understand what I'm saying? It's up to you, it has to be. Do you want me to stay?"

She looked up at him and said one word that caused a warm-fuzzy feeling to tiptoe around her heart and a lovely smile to form on her lips.

Just one little word.

"Yes."

Chapter Eighteen

The small lamp on the nightstand next to the double bed cast a soft glow over the room, and over Tessa and Dominic, who stood naked before each other.

They had entered the house, gone up the stairs and into the bedroom, with an easiness that bespoke an inner knowledge that what was taking place was very right.

In Tessa's room, Dominic had drawn her close and kissed her deeply, causing her to tremble in his arms. Moments later, she'd flipped back the blankets to reveal pristine white sheets.

They'd removed their clothes, then stood statue-still, eyes meeting, then roaming, over the other, savoring all within their view. It was as though there were no world beyond this room. It was a magical night, a Cinderella night, and they were the only two people in the universe.

"You're lovely, Tessa," Dominic said, then extended one hand to her.

She smiled, marveling at her calmness, at the serene sense of knowing who she was and what she wanted. Placing her hand in Dominic's, she stepped into his embrace, relishing the feel of the dark, curly hair on his board chest brushing against the soft flesh of her breasts.

As his mouth captured hers, she drank in his taste while inhaling the aroma that was uniquely his. His strong arms encircled her, held her fast, power tempered with gentleness.

The kiss intensified and heated desire thrummed within them, pulsing, causing hearts to race.

Dominic broke the kiss and lifted Tessa into his arms, placing her on the cool sheets. He reached on the floor for his pants and took a foil packet from his wallet. When he was prepared, he turned to look at her. She lifted her arms to welcome him.

"So beautiful," he murmured, then stretched out next to her, resting on one forearm.

"Dominic," Tessa said, her voice hushed, "it's been so long. My experience is very limited, you see, and I—"

"Shh," he said, then brushed his lips over hers. "Everything will be fine, wonderful."

And it was.

It was a journey of discovery, of touching, kissing, glorying in revealing the mysteries each of the other, rejoicing in the exquisite differences between woman and man, anticipating with ever-growing passion what each would give and receive.

Dominic paid homage to one of Tessa's breasts, then the other, drawing the sweetness deep into his mouth. She purred in pure feminine pleasure.

Her hands were never still as they skimmed over him, feeling the taut muscles beneath her palms. He groaned low in his chest.

Where hands had traveled, lips followed, tongues flicking, tantalizing, heightening desires to a fever pitch of need.

"Oh, Dominic," Tessa whispered.

"I want you, Tessa," he said, his voice gritty.

"Yes."

He filled her with all he was as a man, and she received him joyously with all she was as a woman. In the rhythm ancient as Time itself, yet theirs alone in their special world, the dance of lovers began.

Dominic increased the tempo, and Tessa matched his pace in perfect synchronization. Tension build within them; tighter, hotter, coiling. They were reaching for the summit, going higher, faster, the rhythm now a pounding cadence.

"Dominic!"

Tessa was flung into a place where she had never gone before as she clung to Dominic, calling his name over and over. Rainbow colors burst into glorious pieces like sparkling diamonds.

Moments later, Dominic joined her there, flinging his head back and closing his eyes.

"Tessa."

They stayed in their other-world for moments, or was it forever? Time had no meaning, reality was ecstasy. They were one entity, so totally meshed that in their hearts, minds and souls, there was no discerning one from the other.

It was glorious.

It was beyond anything either of them had ever known before.

Then slowly, quietly, they drifted back, sated, contented, awed by what they'd shared.

Dominic moved off of Tessa, pulled the blankets over them, then nestled her close to his side, one arm wrapped around her waist.

She sighed. "Oh, Dominic, I don't know what to say."

He kissed her on the forehead. "It was incredible. It was . . . I don't know what to say, either."

"Mmm. I'm so sleepy."

"Then sleep. I'll hold you right here in my arms."

"Yes."

As Tessa drifted off into blissful slumber, Dominic frowned.

He felt strange, shaken, unsettled. Making love with Tessa had touched him in a place deep within that he hadn't known existed, nor did he understand what it was. The exquisite physical release was overshadowed by the intensity of emotions very foreign and new, having no names, no identities.

Was this love? Falling in love? How was a man to know? Had this delicate woman sleeping so peacefully in his arms captured his heart? Why did he, a man of experience and intelligence, not know the answers to these questions?

Tessa stirred and he tightened his hold on her, wanting her close to him . . . where she belonged.

Tessa was his now.

With an earthy expletive, he willed himself to blank his mind, *to not think,* not now. He kissed Tessa gently, then slept.

Hours later, as though in a dream, they awakened, reaching for the other, eagerly, urgently. Without speaking, they joined. Without speaking, they traveled yet again to the splendor of the rainbow colors. Without speaking, they savored it all, then allowed sleep to claim them once more.

Tessa opened her eyes, blinked against the bright sunlight that filled the room, then frowned in confusion as she realized she smelled coffee.

"Good morning, Sleeping Beauty," Dominic said.

She turned her head to see him sitting on the edge of the bed.

"Sleeping Beauty?" she said, smiling. "From Cinderella to Sleeping Beauty? I hope my next identity isn't Snow White. I'd really blow my food budget trying to feed those seven guys she hangs out with."

Dominic chuckled, then reached over to the nightstand for one of the two mugs sitting there.

"Coffee?" he said. "I hope you don't mind my making myself at home and fixing a pot."

"Then bringing me a mug in bed? No, I certainly don't mind." She propped her pillow against the headboard, then sat up, tucking the sheet beneath her arms to cover her bare breasts. Accepting the mug from Dominic, she took a sip. "Delicious. Thank you."

Dominic picked up the other mug, then looked directly at Tessa.

"No regrets?" he said, no hint of a smile on his face.

"Oh, no, Dominic, none at all," she said. He looked so ruggedly handsome this morning. He needed a shave, and he was wearing his slacks. He'd slipped on his shirt, but had left it open and hanging free of his pants. The enticing glimpse of his bare chest that was still revealed, caused a frisson of heat to whisper through her. "Do you? Have any regrets?"

"No," he said, then took a swallow of coffee. He could live without the tangled maze of confusion in his weary mind, but he'd tackle that later. "No, Tessa."

Their eyes met again, and the ember of desire still smoldering deep within them burst into flames. Dominic tore his gaze from Tessa's and glanced at the clock.

"It's after nine," he said.

"You're kidding. Goodness, I can't remember when I've slept so late. Little boys are human alarm clocks even on weekends."

"Jason isn't coming home until this evening, is he?"

"No."

"Well, I thought we could spend the day shopping for furniture."

Tessa frowned. "Furniture?"

"Yes. It may take more than one outing to redo this place, but we could get started on it. What room do you want to do first?"

Tessa reached over and placed her mug on the nightstand. Her frown was very much in evidence when she looked at Dominic again.

"I don't recall a discussion regarding new furniture," she said.

"I'm sure I mentioned it." He shrugged. "Maybe not, though. It doesn't matter. It goes with the package of fixing up your house. Things are progressing nicely so far, but there's still furniture and carpeting to do. I'm considering having the road leading in here blacktopped. It's murder on vehicles the way it is. Do you think Jason would like to have bunk beds so he could have a friend sleep over?"

"Wait a minute, Dominic," Tessa said. She raised one hand in a halting gesture, then quickly dropped it as the sheet began to slip. "I don't want new furniture. What I have isn't very expensive, but I saved for each piece, bought it used, then painted, scrubbed, fixed everything up. I'm proud of my purchases."

"What you've done is very admirable, Tessa, but that was then, and this is now. Jason is my son. I want him to have... well, better than this. It's my responsibility."

A cold fist tightened in Tessa's stomach, and she could feel the color drain from her face.

"Responsibility?" she said. "Dear heaven, we're back to responsibility? Or was I wrong to assume that being with Jason, with me, had moved you away from that arena into one of caring?"

Dominic matched her frown. "What I may feel has nothing to do with the fact that I intend to replace our furniture. I don't understand what you're getting upset about."

"No, I realize you have no idea what's bothering me," she said, her voice rising. "Good Lord, I'm sick of hearing you talk about your responsibility. How do you think I feel right now, right this minute, Dominic?"

"Tessa, what in the hell is the matter with you?"

"I'll be only too happy to tell you, Mr. Bonelli. You just spent the night in my bed, remember? We made love. Or did we? Maybe that was just plain old sex, a roll in the hay. It would certainly seem so, because in the light of the new day, you're ready to whip out your checkbook and buy me new furniture."

Dominic thudded his mug onto the nightstand and got to his feet.

"One has nothing to do with the other," he said, matching her volume. "What we shared here—" he swept one arm in the direction of the bed "—is separate and apart from my responsibility for my son. A Bonelli does *not* live in a house with shabby furniture. You're twisting things around, Tessa. You're looking for trouble that isn't there. Being with you has nothing to do with providing material possessions for you and Jason."

"How can you do that? How can you separate your emotions into compartments to suit your fancy? Jason and I aren't robots who need sprucing up. You can't deal with us the way you would when you have your car washed."

"Tessa, stop it. You're being ridiculous. We agreed on this project of fixing your home long before you and I became lovers. One has nothing to do with the other."

Tessa scrambled to her knees, dragging the sheet with her to keep herself covered. Unwelcome tears filled her eyes, but she ignored them.

"You're wrong, Dominic Bonelli. You're so hung up on responsibility, you don't have room for anything else, any other emotions. You actually believe you can interact with me and my son, *my son*, take whatever you want from us, then chalk us up as responsibilities and write a check to cover it."

"Now look—"

"No, you look *and* listen, for a change. I've had enough of your controlling my life, marching in here and barking orders about what will be done to make *my* home meet *your* standards. Jason adores you and I love you and, by damn, you're not going to deal with our existence for one second longer with your crummy money."

"You what?" he said, his voice suddenly very low and very quiet. "You love me?"

"No! Don't be an idiot. I never said..." Tessa voice trailed off, and her eyes widened in horror. "Oh, merciful saints," she whispered.

She *had* said it...well, yelled it. She'd declared her love for Dominic because...because it was true. She *was* in love with him. Oh, darn. Oh, damn. What a stupid thing to have gone and done.

"Tessa?"

"Forget it," she said, shaking her head. "Just forget it. It's not important. That's not the issue here. We're discussing your lamebrain attitude of thinking that your money, your sense of *responsibility,* is all you need to be part of people's lives. That may work with some, but not with me and, by God, not with my son.''

Two tears spilled onto her pale cheeks.

''Get out of my house, *my home,* Dominic Bonelli. You can't possibly be comfortable here, anyway, surrounded by such shabby furniture. Stay away from me, and don't you dare come near Jason again. He honestly believes that you're his friend, that you care about him. Little does he know that your caring is measured in dollars and cents. I won't allow you to break that child's heart. Go. Now!''

Dominic opened his mouth to retort, then snapped it closed again, clenching his jaw in anger. He gathered his remaining clothes, and strode toward the door. He stopped in the doorway and turned to look at Tessa.

''You can't keep me from my son, Tessa,'' he said. ''If I decide to see Jason, I will. No one tells me what I can, or can't do. *No one.* I *do* have a responsibility toward Jason, and I'll see it through to its proper end. Whether that suits your concept of how I should conduct myself is of no importance to me. You can pass judgment on me from here to Sunday, Tessa Russell, but don't expect me to give a tinker's damn one way or another.''

He turned again and left the room, his heavy footsteps on the stairs echoing through the house moments later.

''Dominic?'' Tessa said to the empty room. A sob caught in her throat.

Trembling, she shifted to curl beneath the blankets, her fingertips pressed to her lips.

He was gone. She'd sent him away. In the same moment she'd discovered she'd fallen in love with him, she'd ordered him out of her house and her life.

Why couldn't Dominic see that money wasn't the answer to everything? That responsibility wasn't synonymous with love?

Oh, what difference did it make? He didn't love her. He didn't love Jason. They were simply items on a list to be tended to.

She was a foolish, foolish woman. She'd let down her guard, stepped from behind her protective walls, and would now pay the price with a shattered heart. Once again, she'd fallen in love with the wrong man.

Chapter Nineteen

On Monday afternoon, Dominic stood in his office staring out the window. His hands were shoved into his pockets, and a deep frown knit his eyebrows.

He was, yet again, replaying in his mind everything that had taken place at Tessa's on Sunday morning.

No, that wasn't quite accurate. He was also, despite his attempts to the contrary, reliving Saturday night as well. The memory of the hours at the restaurant then the incredible lovemaking shared with Tessa haunted him, and were now intertwined with the horrendous blowup they'd had.

"Damn," he muttered.

How was it possible that a man could get into so much trouble by suggesting an outing as simple a shopping to buy new furniture? When dealing with woman, that was how. Tessa had been irrational an

stubborn. She had refused to listen to reason; she had
twisted things around in every direction except the one
that was right.

Man, oh, man, she'd been furious.

And sad.

Dominic stared up at the ceiling, seeing in his mind's
eye the tears glistening in Tessa's eyes, then slipping
down her pale cheeks.

Surely she knew that their lovemaking had been exactly that...*making love*. It hadn't been remotely close
to being casual sex—a roll in the hay, as she'd put it.
It had, in fact, been more meaningful than anything
he'd experienced before.

Damn it, why couldn't she get a handle on the facts
as they stood, as he'd explained them to her? His sense
of responsibility toward Jason, toward Tessa herself,
were far removed from what he and Tessa shared.
What was so difficult to comprehend about that concept? It made perfect sense to *him*.

*You're so hung up on responsibility, you don't have
room for anything else, any other emotions.*

Tessa's words hammered against Dominic's mind as
he shifted his gaze to stare once again out the window. A painful headache began to throb in his temples.

Suddenly, he heard the echo of what his mother had
said at that fateful family meeting, and later, when
he'd taken her to lunch.

*Responsibility isn't love. Money isn't love. Are we
the cause of your not knowing the difference between
love and responsibility?*

What do you want?

What do you want?

Dominic ran one hand over the back of his neck.

As long as he was going straight out of his mind, he might as well do it up royally, pull out all the stops, square off against what he'd been trying to ignore.

Tessa Russell loved him.

Emotions slammed against him with such intensity that he took a sharp breath. But the emotions were a tangled maze, twisting and turning, making it impossible to decipher one from the next. Nothing was clear. *Nothing.*

A light knock sounded at the door, then Gladys entered. Dominic turned, grateful for the distraction, for the chance to escape from his own tormented thoughts.

"These letters are ready for your autograph," Gladys said.

He moved behind his desk, sat down and began to sign his name to the pile of letters.

"You're very quiet today," Gladys said.

"I have a lot on my mind."

"Do you want to talk about it?"

"No."

"You never do, Dominic. It can help to talk things through, put it out where you can see it more clearly."

"That wouldn't solve anything in this case, Gladys, but I appreciate the offer." He handed her the letters. "There you go. Thank you."

"You're welcome." She started toward the door.

"Gladys."

She stopped and looked at him over one shoulder. "Yes?"

"Would you leave the door open, please?"

She marched back to stand in front of his desk.

"That corks it," she said. "You've gone over the dge. Leave the door *open?* Dominic, talk to me. ou're not a well man. Either that, or you're not ominic Bonelli at all. Your body has been invaded by lien creatures.

"You *never* want your office door left open. You old the world at bay with the symbolism of that osed door, as well as providing a private place for ourself where you control who enters."

"I never said any of that," he said, frowning up at r.

"I figured it out for myself because I'm an ex- emely intelligent woman. Are you going to try to tell e I'm wrong?"

He opened his mouth to do exactly that, then apped it closed, shook his head and sighed.

"No," he said wearily, "I'm not, because you're ght."

"And now?" she said gently. "Is it finally time to low some of that world out there into your life?"

"Maybe. I don't know, Gladys, but . . . maybe."

"I hope so, Dominic, I truly do."

He leaned back in his chair and laced his fingers hind his head.

"Gladys, humor me. If you had to give a defini- n of the difference between love and responsibility, at would you say?"

"That's easy enough. Love comes from the heart, sponsibility from the mind."

"Don't you think it's more complicated than that?"

"Nope. Would you like an example?"

He nodded.

"Okay. Suppose it's my birthday. If someone buy
me a gift out of a sense of responsibility—you know
with an attitude of *this is something I should do*—the
that gift wouldn't be worth much to me. But if it'
given out of love, then it's very, very precious."

"Oh."

"My phone is ringing." She hurried from the room
leaving the door *open*.

"Love comes from the heart," Dominic said aloud
"responsibility from the mind. It can't be that sim
ple." He paused. "Can it?"

He was an attorney who dealt in concrete fact:
proven data. A theory had now been placed in fro
of him for his consideration. Well, a thought, opir
ion, idea, *anything* would be an improvement over th
tangled maze of confusion in his brain.

*Love comes from the heart, responsibility from th
mind.*

Tessa Russell loved him.

What do you want?

Dominic lunged to his feet.

Enough. He was going crazy. He *had* to find ar
swers to the questions plaguing him, and he'd bett
do a damn good job of it.

Because he knew, just somehow knew that the co
clusions he came to were going to have a tremendor
impact on his future.

A half hour later, Dominic stood in a florist sh
being smiled at by a grandmotherly-type woman.

"How may I help you, sir?" the grandmother-ty
said.

"I'd like to send a bouquet of fresh flowers to my mother."

"Certainly. Did you have something particular in mind? Is it a special occasion?"

"No, it's not," he said, leaning slightly toward her to more clearly analyze her reaction. "That's the point. I'm sending her flowers simply because I want to, because I feel like it."

"Oh-h-h," the woman said, beaming. "What a loving thing to do."

Dominic straightened and blinked. "It is?" He nodded, then smiled, appearing rather pleased with himself. "Well, yes, I guess it is."

The next morning, Carmen opened the door to her studio to find Dominic standing in front of her.

"Dominic?" she said. "What's wrong? Why are you here?"

He frowned. "May I come in?"

"Oh, yes, of course." She stepped back to allow him to enter, then closed the door after him. "Now tell me what's wrong."

He flung out his arms. "Why does something have to be wrong for me to have come here?"

She planted her hands on her hips and glared at him. "Because you don't make social calls on members of your family, big brother. You never have, so why would you start now?"

"Oh," he said, running one hand over the back of his neck. "You're right. I don't just drop by to see how you are, do I?"

"No."

"I certainly am a nice guy," he said dryly.

Carmen cocked her head to one side and studied him. "Are you feeling okay?"

"No, as a matter of fact, I'm not." He paused. "Would you answer a question for me?"

"Sure."

"Why did you paint the rainbow on Tessa's wall?"

"Huh?"

"The rainbow, Carmen, why did you paint it? You took time out from your busy schedule, used expensive supplies, the whole nine yards. Why?"

She shrugged. "Because I like Tessa very much, and Jason is a heart-stealer. I thought they'd enjoy seeing the rainbow every day. It was something I could do for them that might bring some pleasure to their lives."

"I see. Were you registering a sense of responsibility toward them? You know, they're part of the family now so you should do something for them?"

"Responsibility? Heavens no, it never crossed my mind." She splayed one hand across her heart. "I did it because it felt right."

"Man, oh, man, that is really incredible." He gave her a quick kiss on the forehead. "Thanks, Carmen. Bye." He hurried out the door.

Carmen pressed one fingertip to the spot on her forehead where Dominic had kissed her.

"How am I going to break it to our mother," she said aloud, "that her oldest son is no longer playing with a full deck?"

The next evening after work, Dominic stood in the department store where he'd purchased Jason's cowboy suit. He stared at the rack of similar outfits, having told two different saleswomen that he was just browsing.

He mentally took himself back in time to when he'd gotten the bright red suit for Jason.

Why had he done it? It had been on impulse, not something he'd thought through before taking action, which was definitely out of character for him.

How had he felt when he'd given the gift to Jason? Sensational. He'd never forget how that little boy's face had lit up, the way his dark eyes had sparkled with excitement. What a job he and Tessa had had trying to get Jason to stand still long enough to change his clothes. Oh, yes, he was keeping that memory he'd shared with his son.

He'd bought Jason the cowboy suit with a sense of caring...of love. Responsibility hadn't entered into the action one iota.

Dominic took a deep breath, let it out slowly, then wandered away from the boys' department. He was shaken, unsettled, yet, inching in around the edges was a warmth, a strange peacefulness that was increasing with every beat of his racing heart.

"May I help you, sir?"

"What?" he said, jerking in surprise. Glancing around, he discovered he was now in the women's dresses section. "Oh, no, thanks. I'm just looking."

"That's fine, and do let me know if I may be of assistance."

Dominic nodded as his gaze fell on a dress the same color of blue that Tessa had worn when they had gone to dinner.

Tessa, his mind hummed.

Why had he asked her to go out with him on Saturday night? Because he'd wanted to be with her, pure and simple. He'd hollered that fact at her in front of his entire family in his mother's backyard and, by damn, he'd meant it. Responsibility had had nothing to do with it.

And why had he made love with Tessa Russell?

He dragged both hands down his face and felt beads of sweat on his forehead.

He'd *made* love with Tessa, because...because he was *in* love with Tessa.

He stood still, hardly breathing, allowing the truth to move through his mind, his heart, his very soul.

"Yes," he said, a smile breaking across his face. "I'll be damned...yes."

In the next instant, he frowned.

Tessa loved him and he loved her. The problem, however, was that if he showed up on her doorstep, she'd probably deck him. She was, with just cause, mad as hell at him.

And she was sad.

Lord, he'd hurt her so badly. He hadn't meant to, but that fact didn't erase the tears he'd caused to fill her beautiful brown eyes.

He had to regroup, think, plan. He had to win back his lady, the woman he loved.

Tessa was his now.

"Yes!" he said, punching one fist in the air.

"Sir?" a saleswoman said, eyeing him warily.

"What? Oh, it was nice talking to you." He spun on his heel and strode away.

"Weird," the woman muttered. "Gorgeous, but definitely weird."

* * *

Around midnight that night, Tessa awakened from a deep sleep; a small finger was steadily poking her on the arm.

"Jason?" she said foggily.

"Mommy, I don't feel good," he said in a whining voice. "My head hurts. I'm hot. My tummy is wiggling."

"Oh, dear," Tessa said, throwing back the blankets. She snapped on the lamp on the nightstand. "It sounds as though the chicken pox Jeremiah shared with you have finally decided to arrive." She got to her feet.

"My tummy is wiggling worse, Mommy."

"Come on, sweetheart, let's hurry to the bathroom." She paused. "Oh, darn, too late."

The next morning, Jason was covered in a generous display of chicken pox. He was running a slight fever, had no interest in breakfast and was not in a sunshine mood.

Despite Tessa's cheerful account of all the kids from Rainbow's End who had caught chicken pox from Jeremiah so far, Jason seemed to take his case of the polka dots as a personal affront.

"There you go, Mr. Grumpy," she said, tucking Jason in on the cot in her office. "Try to go back to sleep. I'll pop in and out as often as I can. Okay?"

"No. I want to play."

"Not today, my sweetie. You're not going to feel up to snuff until all the chicken pox have come from the inside to the outside. That's how it works."

"That's dumb."

"Your opinion is duly noted." She kissed him on the forehead. "Now then, I've put this little table right next to you here. Try to drink your orange juice, Jason. There are books, crayons, a coloring pad, all kinds of things for you to do. You look sleepy, though. I think you'll snooze if you close your eyes."

"Really, really dumb."

"Got it. I'm going to straighten up the kitchen before the kids start coming, then I'll check on you."

Jason sighed dramatically.

Tessa rolled her eyes heavenward, curbed a smile she decided Jason wouldn't appreciate and left the room. In the kitchen, she set about clearing away the remains of their breakfast.

Poor Jason, she mused. Chicken pox was a miserable thing to go through. She had a feeling he wasn't going to be one bit impressed by Joe's enthusiastic report that someone with the itchy disease looked like birthday cake when covered with the necessary pink lotion.

She was going to be very busy for the next couple of days until Jason began to feel perkier. She'd have to dash back and forth between her regular duties at Rainbow's End and the office where the grouchy patient was.

Well, she'd look at the bright side. Maybe all that busy, busy, busy would mean she wouldn't have time to think about Dominic.

Oh, dear heaven, she thought as she wiped off the table, she loved him. She'd fallen in love with Dominic. The remembrance of the lovemaking they'd shared caused heat to swirl within her, and a flush to stain her cheeks.

The dinner out, dancing, the Cinderella night, had been glorious, too, creating memories she intended to keep for all time.

But then the next morning had arrived, and the chilling argument with Dominic had erupted. She'd been so hurt when he'd shifted back into his responsibility mode, had begun barking orders and taking control of her life.

It would be a cold day in a hot place before she'd allow Dominic to buy her new furniture because hers was too shabby for Jason, a Bonelli, his son, to use. The nerve of that man.

His damnable "responsibility" had seemed to encompass everything they'd shared, *including* the exquisite lovemaking of the night before. She'd lashed out at him so cruelly with her awful remark about him producing his checkbook after spending the night in her bed.

She'd been wrong to say that because she knew in her heart that they *had* made love, not just engaged in casual sex. Dominic had been moved by their union, she was certain of that. Those hateful words she'd hurled at him should never have been spoken.

Tessa sighed and stared out the window over the sink.

Even if she went to Dominic and apologized for saying what she had, nothing would *really* be solved. Yes, they'd made love, but it wasn't enough. The cold, painful truth would remain the same—Dominic's sense of responsibility toward Jason *and* her was far greater than the caring she'd hoped was growing.

She loved Dominic, but he did *not* love her.

Quick tears filled Tessa's eyes and she blinked them away with an angry shake of her head.

Responsibility.

Oh, how she hated that word.

"Blak," she said, then headed for the front door as she heard the sound of children's voices.

Late the next morning, Carmen called Tessa.

"I won't keep you a second," Carmen said. "I know you're busy with the kids. Tomorrow is Saturday, though. That's play-day in my book. Could you and Jason come into town and have lunch with me?"

"Oh, Carmen, that sounds like fun," Tessa said, "but we can't. Jason has chicken pox."

"No joke? How grim. Does he feel awful?"

"He's not up to par yet. He's still running a slight fever and has no pep. I'm holding him prisoner on the cot in my office. He's not a happy camper." She laughed. "He's starting to feel well enough to be showing signs of being a B.I.T."

"A what?"

"Brat-in-training."

Carmen laughed. "I love it. Well, give him a smooch for me. We'll go to lunch another time."

"Thanks for the invitation, Carmen. Bye for now."

Carmen replaced the receiver, narrowed her eyes, then snatched up the receiver again. Moments later she was asking Gladys to put her through to Dominic.

"He's swamped today, Carmen," Gladys said. "And his mood is blacker than coal dust."

"I'll risk it."

"You Bonellis are a brave bunch. Hold on and I'll buzz him."

Carmen tapped her fingertips on the wall next to her telephone.

"What is it, Carmen?" Dominic said gruffly.

"Happy Friday to you, too," she said. "I'm in the mood to go out to lunch tomorrow. Want to join me? In all honesty, you're second choice. I invited Tessa and Jason, but they couldn't go. Poor little Jason is so sick. Anyway, I thought you might—"

Dominic stiffened in his chair. "Jason is sick? What's wrong with him? Why wasn't I told?"

"My stars, Dominic, don't get stressed out. He only has chicken pox. It's just that he's stuck in Tessa's office, he has a slight fever and he's generally not pleased with life. Tessa must be a wreck trying to tend to him as well as take care of things at Rainbow's End. Dominic, do you want to have lunch with me tomorrow, or not?"

"What? Oh, no, I can't. Thanks. Goodbye."

Carmen smiled at the dial tone, then replaced the receiver.

"Gotcha, big brother," she said, giving the telephone a friendly pat.

An hour and a half later, as Tessa was reading the after-lunch story to the children, she heard a car approaching the house. She continued to read, deciding she'd find out who was there when he or she got to the door. The attention of her audience was lost as the screen door was opened. She turned her head and her eyes widened.

"Hello, Tessa," Dominic said.

Chapter Twenty

Tessa forgot to breathe.

The sight of Dominic standing only a few feet awa
stole the very breath from her body. It wasn't until sh
attempted to return his greeting that she realized sh
was completely out of air. She filled her lungs an
strove for a pleasant, casual tone of voice.

"Hello," she said.

She got to her feet, nearly cheering aloud when h
trembling legs actually supported her.

Oh, Dominic, her mind hummed. He appeared
distinguished in his attorney uniform, so rugged
handsome, and she loved him so very much. He w
there, close, yet they were worlds apart.

Yes, Dominic was there but . . . why?

"We're in the middle of story hour," she said. "W
there something in particular that you wanted?"

You, Dominic mentally yelled. He was gazing at the woman he loved, the *only* woman he had ever loved and would love for all time. He wanted Tessa, needed her in his life to make him whole. He needed her, and Jason, his son, and the babies he and Tessa would create together in the future.

"Dominic?"

He cleared his throat. "Yes. I'm here to see Jason. I spoke with Carmen and she said he has chicken pox, so I drove out to spend some time with him."

Tessa frowned. "In the middle of your workday?"

"Gladys, my secretary, may never speak to me again because she had to reschedule a very full calendar for this afternoon but... May I see Jason?"

"Yes, of course. He's in my office."

"Fine. You just go on with what you were doing." He paused. "Oh, I hope you don't mind, but I gave Gladys your telephone number. I was waiting for some important information and if it reaches her, I'll have to tell her how to proceed, depending on what she learns."

Tessa nodded, then watched as Dominic crossed the room and disappeared into the kitchen.

Did this make sense? she asked herself, totally confused. Dominic had left his office in the middle of an extremely busy day to come to see Jason? No, that did not make sense. Where was his ever-famous sense of responsibility? He was an attorney with obligations and *responsibilities,* for heaven's sake.

"Are you gonna finish the story?" Jeremiah said, bringing Tessa back from her reverie.

"The what?" she said. "Oh! The story." She sat back down. "Okay, where were we?"

The story hour was finally completed, much t
Tessa's relief. Jeremiah had pointed out, none too
happily, that Tessa had read the same page twice on
three occasions before finishing the book.

Emma and Patty emerged from the kitchen to take
the children to the play yard. Both women looked a
Tessa questioningly.

"That's Dominic," Tessa said, picking an imagi
nary thread from her blouse. "He's one of the Bonel
lis. You know, the group that's been tromping in an
out of here repairing the house."

Emma giggled. "Was Dominic the grand prize i
the contest?"

"Contest?" Tessa said.

"The Fix-Up-Your-House contest that you won."

"Oh, *that* contest," Tessa said, nodding. "I re
member that contest. That was really something
wasn't it?" She pressed one hand to her forehead
"Ignore me."

"Why do I get the feeling there's more going on he
than meets the eye?" Emma said.

"Because there is," Patty said firmly. "Let's g
these darlings outside and leave Tessa to do what sl
needs to do."

"Prepare the afternoon snack," Tessa said quickl

"And whatever," Patty said, beaming. "Let's g
little ones. Put your story rugs in the pile where th
belong, then we're off to play."

Much too soon to suit Tessa's frazzled nerves, sl
was alone, the sound of happy children reaching h
from the play yard.

She took a steadying breath, squared her shou
ders, then went, albeit rather slowly, to the doorw:

f the office. Tears burned at the back of her eyes as he drank in the sight before her.

Dominic had removed his jacket and tie, undone the wo top buttons of his shirt and rolled the sleeves to midforearm. He was sitting on the side of the cot, an pen storybook balanced on his knees. Jason had allen asleep and Dominic was looking at him, simply ooking at him, one of Jason's small hands cradled in Dominic's large one.

Dominic and Jason, Tessa thought, her heart racng. The two most important people in her world, the wo she loved with all that she was.

The telephone rang and both Tessa and Dominic rked at the sudden noise. Tessa turned to hurry to he wall telephone in the kitchen, hoping the shrill ring f the one on her desk wouldn't waken Jason.

''Rainbow's End,'' she said into the receiver.

''Tessa? This is Gladys, Dominic's secretary. May I peak with him, dear?''

''Yes, I'll get him.''

''I'm here,'' he said from directly behind her.

He took the receiver from Tessa.

''Yep?...I see...That's good. Call Jamison and ll him we're a go, Gladys, that the report came in ith what we wanted...Who?...Oh, hell, Baxter? e didn't have an appointment...Yes, I realize I queeze him in if he comes to town unexpectedly, but ot this time...No, he won't be happy, but those are e breaks. What I'm doing here is more important to e...Yes, you can have a raise as compensation for ombat duty...Goodbye, Gladys.''

He replaced the receiver and turned to see Tessa aring at him with a shocked expression on her face.

"Dominic," she said, wringing her hands, "I think perhaps you've misunderstood chicken pox. What mean is, Jason isn't seriously ill. He's grumpy and a tad uncomfortable, that's all. There's no reason fo you to disrupt your work schedule and upset an im portant client."

He shrugged. "Don't worry about it."

"Don't worry about it?" she repeated. "Good grief Dominic, I don't want Jason to be the cause of you ignoring your responsibilities at your office."

"My responsibilities," Dominic said slowly. "Tha word has played a major part in my life. In fact, it ha been front-row center in the spotlight, hasn't it?" H folded his arms across his chest. "As I recall, you'r the one who was very vocal on the subject of my plac ing far too much emphasis on responsibility."

"Oh. Well, yes, I was, but darn it, Dominic, you'r confusing me."

"Then by all means, Tessa, allow me to explain."

He dropped his arms to his sides and started to ward her. Tessa began to back up, frantically searcl ing his face for some clue as to his mood, his frame c mind and failing to decipher a thing.

He came close. She moved farther back. She f nally thudded against the refrigerator. Dominic brace one hand on either side of her head, trapping her i place. Her heart pounded as she stared up at him.

"Tessa," he said, his voice low, "I've spent mar hours going over everything that transpired betwee us. Everything."

A warm flush crept onto Tessa's cheeks as images the lovemaking shared with Dominic flickered into h mind's eye. She willed the tantalizing pictures to *go away*.

"Responsibility," Dominic said, then shook his head. "It was all I'd known for so long that it was a way of life to me. I was *responsible* for a great many people who needed food and a roof over their heads. Later, the needs changed, and I saw to those too. It was up to me."

"You did a wonderful job all those years for your family," she said, her voice hushed.

"To a point, only to a point. I've come to see, Tessa, because of you, and Jason, that there's more that should be given than just money, opportunities, material things. I left out a very important ingredient."

"You did?"

"I did. I didn't reach deep enough within myself to find, then give, *love*. Until you. Until Jason."

"What . . . what are you saying, Dominic?"

"Responsibility comes from the mind. Love comes from the heart."

"Yes, Dominic, I know."

"So do I . . . now. I'm here today because I *want* to be here. Responsibility has nothing to do with it. *It feels right*. I'm here to ask you to forgive me for hurting you. I didn't mean to cause you to cry, Tessa, but I know I did, and I'm so damn sorry."

"I . . ."

"And I'm here," he went on, "to tell you *from my heart*, that I love you. I am in love with you, Tessa, and I hope, pray, you'll agree to be my wife. We'll raise Jason, *our son*, together and, God willing, we'll add some more babies to the clan."

Tears filled Tessa's eyes.

"Ah, hell, Tessa," Dominic said, his voice choked with emotion. "I've been so wrong about this responsibility thing for so long. I'll need you to be patient with me until I really get a solid handle on how it's supposed to work."

Two tears slid down Tessa's cheeks.

"Don't cry," he said. "I don't know what to do when you cry. Are you sad again? I love you, I want to spend the rest of my life with you. Am I too late? Are you beyond being able to forgive me? Is that why you're crying?"

"Oh, no, Dominic," she said, placing her hands on his cheeks. "These are tears of joy because I love you so much. I thought you were lost to me."

A sob caught in her throat.

"Yes, oh, yes, I'll marry you," she said, smiling through her tears. "The future looked so bleak, so lonely, without you. You were the treasure at the end of my rainbow that I believed I would never have. I love you, Dominic Bonelli."

Dominic closed his eyes for a moment and took a raspy breath.

"Thank God," he said, his voice thick with emotion. He looked directly into Tessa's eyes again. "And I love you, Tessa Russell."

He pulled her close, his mouth melting over hers as she moved her hands from his face to entwine them around his neck.

The kiss was searing, causing desire to consume them. The kiss was forgiveness and greater understanding. The kiss was happiness filling their hearts and sealing their commitment to forever.

"Mommy? Dominic?" Jason had left the office and was standing in the kitchen doorway yawning. "Dominic, when you're done doin' that kissing stuff with my mom, would you read more of the story to me?"

"Kissing stuff?" Dominic said with a burst of laughter. "Remind me to ask you how you feel about kissing stuff in about ten years, Jason." He looked at Tessa. "Should we talk to him now about our future?"

Tessa nodded. "Yes, but I don't think this is the time to explain everything. When he's older, we'll tell him about Janice. Is that all right?"

"It's fine, just fine."

They crossed the room and Dominic picked Jason up, giving him a hug. The trio went into the office and settled onto the cot, Jason nestled on Dominic's lap.

"Jason," Dominic said, "you and I are friends, right?"

"Right."

"Friends like each other, right?"

"Right."

"Well, my feelings for you grew bigger than just liking you as a friend. I love you, Jason, and I love your mother, very, very much. I've asked your mom to marry me, to be my wife."

"Oh," Jason said, frowning. "Does that mean my mom is the mom, and you're the dad, and I'm the little boy?" His face lit up with a smile. "Are we going to be a family, really for honest?"

"Really for honest," Dominic said. "Does that sound okay to you?"

Jason placed his small hands on Dominic's cheeks. "Are you gonna be my daddy?"

"Oh, yes, Jason," he said, tears filling his eyes. "I'm going to be the best daddy I can possibly be."

"Will you love me and my mom forever?"

"Forever and an extra day."

"*Buono!*" Jason yelled, then flung his arms around Dominic's neck.

"Oh-h-h," Tessa said, smiling even as tears spilled onto her cheeks.

"Jason," Dominic said, "this means that *all* the Bonellis will be part of your family for that forever and an extra day. How does *that* sound?"

"Neato!" Jason wiggled off Dominic's lap. "Wait, wait."

He rummaged through a stack of papers, took one, grabbed a roll of tape from Tessa's desk and ran out of the room.

Tessa and Dominic looked at each other questioningly, then got quickly to their feet to follow Jason.

In the main room, Jason taped the paper he'd colored to the spot just above the empty pot at the base of the rainbow on the wall.

In the drawing were stick figures of a man, woman and child.

"That's me," Jason said, pointing to the smallest figure. "That's you, Mommy, and that's you, Dominic. I drew that for my rainbow wish, and it came true. That's cool."

Tessa and Dominic looked at each other, love shining in their eyes that glistened with tears.

"It's wonderful," Tessa whispered.

"It's forever," Dominic said.

Jason marched back into the office and busied himself looking at a book.

His mom and dad would read him a story later, he decided, but now they were doin' that kissing stuff again.

In the main room, a sudden burst of sunlight shone through the front window directly onto the glorious rainbow, making the vibrant colors glow even brighter.

Dominic lifted his head to speak close to Tessa's lips. "*Io ti voglio bene.* I love you."

"*Buono,* Dominic," Tessa said, smiling. "*Buono.*"

Epilogue

One Year Later

Dominic crossed the large living room and settled onto the sofa facing a crackling fire in the hearth. He picked up one of Tessa's hands and kissed the palm.

"Is Jason asleep?" Tessa said.

"Out like a light. I read him the Buddy Bunny story again. I can just about recite that one by heart."

Tessa smiled. "It's his favorite, because Buddy Bunny found his family just as Jason feels *he* did. Oh Dominic, Jason is such a happy little boy."

"And you, Mrs. Bonelli? How are you measuring on the happiness scale?"

"Up and over the top."

"Ditto." He gave her a quick kiss on the lips. "I'm sorry I was late getting home. I hate not having dinner with you and Jason."

"It doesn't happen very often, and you do have *responsibilities* at the office, Mr. Bonelli."

Dominic rolled his eyes heavenward. "That word, that word. It will haunt me until I'm old and gray."

"No, I just poke you with it once in a while so we never forget how close we came to not understanding each other, losing what was ours to share. I don't ever want to take our world for granted, Dominic."

"Fair enough. So, sweet wife, what kind of day did you have?"

"Well, the drapes came for our bedroom, so I took the sheets off the windows. I gave Carmen my first official report as a free-lance accountant. The details are worked out for the barbecue here Sunday to celebrate our built-from-scratch new home, with all the Bonellis in attendance. And I signed the papers selling Rainbow's End to the single mother with the two little girls."

Dominic chuckled. "Is that all? We need to talk about how lazy you've become."

Tessa laughed in delight, then her smile faded. "Dominic?"

"Yes, my love?"

"I did one other thing today."

"Oh?" He raised his eyebrows.

"Well, I... Oh, dear," she said, her eyes filling with tears.

"Hey, whoa," he said, encircling her with his arms. "What is it? What's wrong?"

"Nothing is wrong," she said quickly. "You get s[o] upset at the sight of tears."

"Yeah, well, they shake me up. Confess. What els[e] did you do today?"

"I found out that we're going to have a baby."

Dominic opened his mouth, snapped it closed, the[n] tried again.

"Are you sure?" he said. "Jeez, Bonelli, that wa[s] dumb. Of course you're sure. Oh, Tessa, that is far[n] tastic. You're pleased, aren't you? I'd hate to b[e] floating around on cloud nine all alone."

"I'm thrilled, Dominic. There aren't words to te[ll] you how happy I am."

"Ah, Tessa, thank you. I love you, I love you, I lov[e] you."

He kissed her deeply, and their passion soared in[-] stantly, burning like the licking flames in the fir[e] place.

They stood only long enough to shed their clothe[s] then sank onto the plush carpeting, the fire's lig[ht] casting a golden glow over their naked bodies.

It was all so familiar, yet, in the wondrous world [of] lovers who were truly in love, it was new and excitin[g]

Dominic splayed one hand across Tessa's stomac[h]

"Hello, little Bonelli," he said, his voice husky wi[th] emotion. "Hello, little miracle. You've got a danc[e] big brother, who's going to think you're the greate[st] thing since *gelato*."

"Do you hope it's a girl?" Tessa said.

"That would be nice. We'd have a son and daughter. Or we'll have two sons, if it's a boy.

doesn't matter. We'll have two children. Ours. Ours, Tessa."

"Oh, Dominic, I love you so much."

He captured her mouth with his, and they gave way to their desire, hearts nearly bursting with love and the multitude of blessings they knew were theirs.

Hands and lips paid homage to a body soft and a body taut with muscles. They held back, anticipating what was yet to come, until they could wait no more.

Dominic moved over Tessa and entered her. They were one entity—hearts, minds, souls and bodies meshed.

They soared to their place, the private ecstasy that was theirs alone, reaching for it, higher and higher, bursting upon it moments apart as they whispered the name of the one they loved.

They lingered there, surrounded by the glorious colors of the rainbow.

* * * * *

The conclusion to the compelling series
MAN, WOMAN and CHILD is on its way to
you next month. Don't miss
NOBODY'S CHILD by Pat Warren
(Special Edition #974). It's a keeper!

* * *

EXTRA SPECIAL ANNOUNCEMENT

The next time you see **Robin Elliott,** *she'll be
writing under her real name*
Joan Elliott Pickart. *Don't miss the fun! She'll
be in Silhouette Desire in the fall, with a
wonderful new mini-series—THE BABY BET!*

Silhouette®

SPECIAL EDITION

COMING NEXT MONTH

#973 THE BRIDE PRICE—Ginna Gray

That Special Woman!

Wyatt Sommersby couldn't help but be attracted to the passionate Maggie Muldoon. When her free-spirited nature resisted Wyatt's tempting proposal of marriage, it left Wyatt wondering—what would be the price of this bride?

#974 NOBODY'S CHILD—Pat Warren

Man, Woman and Child

Feeling like nobody's child compelled Lisa Parker to search out her true parents. It brought her face-to-face with J. D. Kincaid, a man whose emotional past mirrored her own, and whose tough exterior hid a tender heart....

#975 SCARLET WOMAN—Barbara Faith

Years ago, Clint Van Arsdale watched as his brother eloped with Holly Moran, a girl from the wrong side of the tracks. Now Holly was a widow—yet despite the pain of a shared past, Clint could no longer escape their undeniable attraction.

#976 WHAT SHE DID ON HER SUMMER VACATION—Tracy Sinclair

Melanie Warren's vacation jaunt unexpectedly landed her in an English country manor. When the very proper and very sexy David Crandall invited her to become nanny to his adorable twins, she just couldn't turn him down....

#977 THE LAST CHANCE RANCH—Ruth Wind

Life's hard knocks forced Tanya Bishop to leave her son in the care of strong and sensible Ramon Quezada. Returning home to reclaim her lost child, she didn't count on falling under Ramon's seductive spell.

#978 A FAMILY OF HER OWN—Ellen Tanner Marsh

Sassy Waring's lonely heart longed for that special kind of family she'd only heard about. When Sam Baker came into her and her young niece's life, would she dare hope that her dream could finally come true?

He's Too Hot To Handle...but she can take a little heat.

SILHOUETTE

Summer Sizzlers

This summer don't be left in the cold, join Silhouette for the hottest Summer Sizzlers collection. The perfect summer read, on the beach or while vacationing, Summer Sizzlers features sexy heroes who are "Too Hot To Handle." This collection of three new stories is written by bestselling authors Mary Lynn Baxter, Ann Major and Laura Parker.

Available this July wherever
Silhouette books are sold.

Silhouette

SPECIAL EDITION

™

MAN & Woman & CHILD

Three provocative family tales...three wonderful
writers...all come together in a series destined to win
your heart!

NOBODY'S CHILD
by Pat Warren
SE #974, August 1995

Liza Parker always felt as if she were nobody's child.
Helping her find her true parents was J. D. Kincaid, a
man whose emotional past mirrored her own, and
whose tough exterior hid a tender heart....

Coming in August, don't miss NOBODY'S CHILD,
by Pat Warren. Only from Silhouette Special Edition.

FLYAWAY VACATION SWEEPSTAKES!

This month's destination:

Glamorous LAS VEGAS!

Are you the lucky person wh
will win a free trip to Las Vega
Think how much fun it would l
to visit world-famous casinos
to see star-studded shows...
enjoy round-the-clock action
the city that never sleeps!

The facing page contains two Official Entry Coupor
as does each of the other books you received this sh
ment. Complete and return all the entry coupons
**the more times you enter, the better your chanc
of winning!**

Then keep your fingers crossed, because you'll find c
by August 15, 1995 if you're the winner! If you a
here's what you'll get:

- Round-trip airfare for two to exciting Las Vegas!
- 4 days/3 nights at a fabulous first-class hotel!
- $500.00 pocket money for mea and entertainment!

Remember: The more times you enter, the better your chances of winning!*

*NO PURCHASE OR OBLIGATION TO CONTI
BEING A SUBSCRIBER NECESSARY TO ENTER.
REVERSE SIDE OF ANY ENTRY COUPON
ALTERNATIVE MEANS OF ENTRY.

FLYAWAY VACATION
SWEEPSTAKES
OFFICIAL ENTRY COUPON

This entry must be received by: JULY 30, 1995
This month's winner will be notified by: AUGUST 15, 1995
Trip must be taken between: SEPTEMBER 30, 1995-SEPTEMBER 30, 1996

YES, I want to win a vacation for two in Las Vegas. I understand the prize includes round-trip airfare, first-class hotel and $500.00 spending money. Please let me know if I'm the winner!

Name_____

Address _____Apt. _____

City   State/Prov.   Zip/Postal Code

Account #_____

Return entry with invoice in reply envelope.

© 1995 HARLEQUIN ENTERPRISES LTD.   **CLV KAL**

FLYAWAY VACATION
SWEEPSTAKES
OFFICIAL ENTRY COUPON

This entry must be received by: JULY 30, 1995
This month's winner will be notified by: AUGUST 15, 1995
Trip must be taken between: SEPTEMBER 30, 1995-SEPTEMBER 30, 1996

YES, I want to win a vacation for two in Las Vegas. I understand the prize includes round-trip airfare, first-class hotel and $500.00 spending money. Please let me know if I'm the winner!

Name_____

Address _____Apt. _____

City   State/Prov.   Zip/Postal Code

Account #_____

Return entry with invoice in reply envelope.

© 1995 HARLEQUIN ENTERPRISES LTD.   **CLV KAL**